Freedom: Elle's Story

Tara Fox Hall

Published by
Melange Books, LLC
White Bear Lake, MN 55110
www.satinromance.com

Cover Design by Caroline Andrus

To Holly and Jessica, for all your support (and Misery threats). :) This one's for you.

Chapter One

My name is Elle O'Connor. You probably don't know who I am. But if you're any type of being other than human, you've likely heard of my father, Theopolis. He's what's called a Ranked assassin, which means he has international status. He also happens to be a werecougar, and an asshole most of the time. You might also know about my mom, Sarelle, if you keep track of the who's who of vampires in the United States, as she's been involved with several in the last five years. She's still human, but it's been a near miss kind of situation lately.

Theopolis and I haven't been speaking for most of this year. I was there the night he tried to hurt Mom, and I haven't forgiven him for what he did, to put it mildly. The bald-faced truth is he wasn't much of a father to me. Now that he's mated to another woman, it's not like he has time for me, anyway.

Mom wasn't a great mother, though I understand that wasn't her fault. The story, if you aren't familiar with it, is that Sarelle isn't my biological mother. My biological mother, Tawny, died in childbirth. I never knew her, or even saw a picture of her. But Sarelle tells me that I look a lot like she did, with wavy blonde hair, and blue eyes.

Sarelle is the woman I think of as my mother. She took care of me in the first few months after I was born, when my father disappeared. But she was a wreck herself, as they'd been planning to get married. They had gotten engaged a few nights before he went missing, and it was very dramatic not knowing what had happened to him, or if he was even alive for over a year.

Before she was in love with my father, Sarelle—or Sar, as she likes her friends to call her—she loved a vampire by the name of Danial. It was he who really raised me. I'd met him a few days after I was born, over in Europe, and when he came to see her and me, after he'd come back after months of looking for my missing father, I was very glad to see him again.

Two weeks after Danial came to see Sar that night, she and I moved in with him. I feel like I should defend her decision to do that, as it makes it seem like she didn't love my father, to go and live with another man so quickly. I want you to know that I think that one decision was maybe the best thing she ever did for me. She tried hard to take care of me, but even though I was very young, I could see she was a wreck. I could also tell she was scared: scared of being alone with a non-human baby she didn't know how to care for; scared my father was not coming back, scared of what was going to happen to us. And Danial, with his calm assurance and his vast wealth swept in and fixed everything in a single night. What woman wouldn't have leaned on a man like that, especially as it was easy to see she still loved him?

To say he was a father to me wasn't enough. In those first years he was everything a father should be, and then more. When I was hurt or sad, he was there to kiss and hug away my tears. When I was angry and mean, he was calm and talked to me, teaching me how to handle my anger. And when I was inquisitive, or bored, he was there to tell me the reasons why things were the way they were, or to show me books or other hobbies that not only kept me entertained, but also enriched my mind.

The result of his attention to me was inevitable: I adored him completely. It wasn't long before I called him Dad. And he is still the only one I've ever called Dad.

* * * *

I started college this past January. At first, I really liked it. It was exhilarating to finally be living away from my family, to not have to worry about any guards watching me, to finally have the freedom to do what I wanted when I wanted.

I'd never made friends easily, but I was able to make a bunch in my dorm the first week. They were a lot like Susan, my dance-class friend of a year or so ago, had been. We partied a little, smoked a little grass, and talked about clothes and celebrities.

But there was one recurring problem. These girls all had boyfriends, or at least lovers, and would meet them at least weekly to have sex. I had no desire for a man to touch me at all. The truth was if men weren't related to me, I didn't want them within reach of me. Anytime I was alone with any male, even a teacher, I made whatever excuse I had to in order to leave immediately for my dorm room.

At first, the other girls didn't notice. But after a month, they began telling me they felt sorry for my "celibacy problems," that they knew guys who were single who'd love to have sex with me. Telling them that I wanted to wait for marriage was met with laughs, or outright looks of disbelief. One even sent a guy named Will to my room with some flowers. And when I refused to open the door to him, or even talk to him, what had been something to tease me about abruptly became something that marked me as abnormal.

My so-called "friends" avoided me after that. I told myself it was okay, that I had screwed around for the first month of school, and my average was a C in most classes. I needed time to study if I was going to do well in any of them.

So, for the month of February, I mostly became a hermit. I went to the library, and ate by myself in the food court with a book, and thought about how many more years of this I would be able to stand before I was so lonely I spontaneously combusted.

Part of the problem was that I wasn't sure who to turn to and talk about how I felt. By that time, my father Theo had remarried, and my mother was living with Danial's brother, Devlin.

Again, I feel like I should give some background information. Devlin had been wanting into my mother's underwear from the first time he saw her, back when she was dating Danial. And over the years he'd done a hell of a lot to try to force the issue: kidnapping her, giving her his powerful blood to make her in thrall to him, seducing her, threatening to kill people she cared about, and even staging an elaborate scenario where he saved her from a dangerous gangster with a grudge against her. But my mother was a smart woman, and all his attempts to get her to like him got him nowhere.

This made him mad. And though no one ever has come right out and said this to me, I know that somewhere after that specific scenario was played out, Devlin got her alone somehow, and…and he...he…

Sorry, give me a minute.

* * * *

Sorry about that. I've been going to therapy for almost a year now. And the months have helped to make some of my fear and anger and helplessness go away. But it's still hard to talk about for me. And the reason is that what happened to my mother with Devlin happened to me with another man.

I feel like I should elaborate on what happened, so you don't think it was my parent's fault, because it wasn't. My mother had warned me repeatedly about men, and being careful with them, especially after catching me with a man many years my senior in a…compromising position. My Dad had also told me the same thing. Even Theo had echoed the "be careful around strange men" phrase. If it was anyone's fault that I got in a position to be hurt, it was my own.

The facts are these: almost a year ago, I began sneaking out after dark. My dad Danial was in a coma then and my father Theo was oblivious. Danial's estate was large, with multiple buildings. There were always vehicles parked in the garage, keys under the visor, and people came and went at all hours from the estate, so it was easy. Plus, I knew how to drive from some lessons a former boyfriend of mine, Hans, had given me.

At first, I'd gone to the mall at night, meeting a friend of mine for movies. But my friend Violet was younger than me, and being werecougar, I was maturing fast. I didn't want to talk about My Little Pony, or about High School Musical, I wanted to talk about kissing,

4

and flirt with boys, if not get physical. So pretty soon I stopped telling her I'd be there, and told her I was busy. Soon after, I met a really cute guy in the food court.

To say he was hot didn't cover it. I didn't know then, but an enemy of Devlin's had found out about me being Sar's adopted daughter, and was looking to hurt Devlin through me. So he picked the man of his who might have been a poster child for a young girl's wet dream, and sent him to hang out at the mall, and get close to me, in order to hurt me.

Again, I was the one who pursued him. I kissed him first, and when he didn't push it farther, I did. A few weeks later, when we'd done most everything but intercourse and he suggested going to a motel, I was already standing before he finished talking, telling him I was ready to leave. I remember thinking it was going to be so wonderful, to finally lose my virginity. Instead, I got raped.

Don't feel sorry for me. I've come to a point where I'm okay talking about it. I don't remember any of what actually happened, as I was unconscious. That was and remains a blessing to me. But I'm getting way off track here.

My mother was living with Devlin at the time this happened to me, because she'd broken up with my father, Theo. He wanted her to be werecougar like he and I were, and had asked her to let him change her. She refused, saying to my shock that she loved Lash, a good friend of Devlin's. Theo attacked her in his fury, and she shot him in the heart, and ran to Hayden, Devlin's home. And that was that, or so I thought.

But when I'd attended the wedding of a friend in January, I'd learned from my mother that she'd given Devlin a kind of promise, an Oath, which was kind of a marriage thing for vampires. Not only that, she'd given a mating promise to Lash, too.

Was I upset? Sure. To say I disliked Devlin wasn't strong enough. But I did like Lash, even though he was a weresnake, and I saw how he was with her at the wedding, how attentive, and caring. Lash had saved Mom from other men who'd wanted to hurt her, men like my father. In spite of how nasty his snake scent was to me, I knew I'd never scented another woman on him in all the times I'd seen him since the time he'd met my mother, over a year ago. I couldn't even say that about my Dad or the reverse for my mother. So, I decided that I'd give him a chance, since their relationship seemed to be working, at least so far.

So when I called my mother one day in the second week of February, I prayed that either he or she would answer. To my relief, Lash answered. "Sar's with V," he hissed to me gently. "I'll get her for you."

"Thanks."

"But first tell me how you are," he said in his singular hissing tone. "We haven't seen you since Terian and Sundown's wedding. How is college?"

I'm lonely and am never going to be loved. "Okay."

"Be more descriptive."

I bit my lip. "Why are you asking me this?" I said carefully.

"You are my mate's daughter." His tone was matter of fact.

"I'm also your worst enemy's daughter."

"Don't be like that," he said, annoyed. "Have I ever treated you like a…a…"

"Like a werecougar?" I supplied.

Lash let out a breath. "Well, yes. Your scent is distasteful to me, as I'm sure mine is to you."

"Yes." It was like musty old leaves, dead skin, and mold. I didn't understand how Mom could stand it, even if he was a nice person.

"It's true that most cougars and snakes hate each other," Lash said in a pained tone. "We're natural enemies, just like foxes and coyotes. But I don't hate you. And I don't want you to hate me, even if your father does. Okay?"

"Okay."

"Good. Now tell me how you are."

"I'm good," I said, thinking frantically for something to say that sounded not like a lie, and didn't reveal my utter loneliness. "My classes are interesting. The people seem nice enough. And the nature preserve is large."

"Can you change there?" Lash said, sounding hopeful. "Be careful, and don't let your footprints get seen—"

"I'm not an idiot!" I said a little abruptly. "I don't change on campus. There's a wildlife preserve a half-hour away. I've gone there a few times. There are grouse there, and squirrels, which are big enough to fill my need for meat—"

"Grouse are tasty," Lash hissed, sounding hungry. "I'm looking forward to spring, when I can hunt some for myself again at Hayden. And there'll be eggs then, too."

Being cold-blooded probably curtails his winter hunting. "What do you do in the winter, Lash?"

"Your mother sometimes brings me sushi," Lash hissed affectionately. "And there's always meat, even if cow and chicken tastes bland next to wild game. And if I'm out on a job and it's someplace warm, I sometimes am able to get a few trout, or other types of fish. Fish are my favorite."

I didn't know what to say, knowing what his "job" was. *Killing for cash.* I settled for saying, "I like fish, too."

"Are you coming home for Easter? I understand from Sar that you have a break then?"

"Maybe," I said hesitantly. "It depends. I have finals after, so it might be better if I stayed here and studied. College lets out in May."

"Well, don't study too hard. I, like your mother, want you to succeed. But we want you to be happy most of all."

I felt choked up suddenly. The words he'd said sounded so much like my Dad's. *Dad, who might never be happy again, much less tell*

7

me he wants me to be happy.

"Hold on, Elle. I'll be a few minutes, getting your mother."

I heard him put down the phone, and then nothing.

A half-minute later, the phone was picked up.

"Mom?"

"Elle," a melodious voice crooned in my ear. "How are you doing?"

God, it was Devlin. *Bastard.* "Fine," I said in an icy tone. "I'm waiting to talk to my mom."

"Tell me how you are," he said cajolingly. "Met any nice boys?"

I gave a hitching breath, and gulped a little.

"I'm sorry," he said quickly. "I did not mean to be hurtful, Elle. I just wish to speak to you, to make sure you are well." He paused. "Have you spoken to Danial?"

"Not recently." That was sad but true. But my father had come out of his coma about a month ago. Though he physically was fine, his memories had been altered by his brush with death. In short, he no longer knew who my mother was: he thought Sarelle was dead, and he thought that my mother was a woman called Lady who had usurped my mother's position unfairly. So when I'd last talked to him, he'd been ranting about how my mother was turning in her grave to see Devlin carrying on so soon after her death with another woman. He'd also gone on and on about how much he missed her, damning the demon who had killed her. To bear witness to that overwhelming grief had been draining, especially when none of it was true. So, when days had passed and then a month with no call from Dad, I hadn't picked up the phone to call him.

"Elle, are you still there?"

"Please, Devlin, get my mother, okay?"

"Is something wrong?" he said, immediately alert. "Do you need help?"

"No! I just don't want to talk to you anymore!"

"I know you and I have not got along in the past," he said delicately. "But you are my Oathed One's child, and even if you were not, you are my brother's daughter, no matter that we don't share blood. I would like to mend those fences, if you would permit me to."

"Look, I know what you did to my mom," I growled at him. "But she wants to be with you, so I'm not going to cause problems, especially after what my father tried—"

"What are you talking about?" Devlin said in confusion.

Shit. He doesn't know about Theo trying to change my mom into a werecougar? Lash didn't tell him? Mom didn't?

"Elle, speak," Devlin said, his words heavy with rage. "What did your father do to Sar? I thought she acted more afraid of him than she should!"

"He fought with her, when she told him she cared about Lash. He…he hit her."

"When was this?" His tone was deadly.

"The night she came to you, back in the fall."

"The night Titus broke the love spell on her and him," Devlin murmured thoughtfully. "Was she hurt by his blow? Titus didn't tell me of healing her, and he would have, if she'd come to him with a wound of any kind—"

I couldn't focus on anything but his admission. "There was a love spell on my mom and my father?"

"Terian put it on them by accident years ago. It was done wrong, or so Titus told me." He turned regretful. "It was the reason she went to find Theo and did not stay with my brother, you, and his son, as she was meant to. It's the reason that she went back to him, after all he had put her through."

9

He was talking about when my mother had found out Theo was alive, years ago. She'd left Theoron, Danial's son with her, when he was newly born, and gone off to find him. She'd just abandoned Danial after living with him for almost a year and a half. And she'd left me, too. I'd always felt bad about that. Hearing this made me feel a little better; he was saying it hadn't been her decision, a spell on her had made her go to him and leave us.

"That spell is broken now," Devlin said. "Sar is here with me, as she should be. Lash, as you know, is also mated to her. There were no bad lasting effects."

Except perhaps to my mother, for knowing she had no real say in what she was doing. But maybe that makes her feel better, to know she wasn't as heartless as she seemed then. "I know."

"Good. Now tell me, was your mother hurt by Theo's blow?" That rage was back in his words.

"No," I lied, thinking quickly. "I think she might have bit her tongue, but that was all. I didn't see it, I just heard a slap."

"Then I'll let it go, and say nothing," Devlin said, his anger fading from his voice. "It may be more painful for her to remember that night than the actual slap was."

I didn't reply. It wasn't my place to tell him any of this, if my Mom hadn't.

"Your mother has offered that you live with us," he continued. "And you've refused. So I want to offer it to you again, on the off chance you thought I would not welcome you if you—"

"I don't like you," I growled at him. "I don't want to live with you!"

"What about Danial?" he asked, again manipulative. "You know he lives here now, too. You know he loves you, Elle. He would welcome you to Hayden with open arms—"

"Devlin, I need this time to be on my own, to be alone," I growled. "I have never been on my own, do you understand?"

"No, I do not," he said, confused. "I do not like to be alone, and I was for many years, before meeting your mother. Being alone is overrated. It is for asexual beings, and those who are too ugly for anyone to consider being intimate with."

My God, he is insufferable! How does my mother stand him? I was about to hang up the phone when my mother came on, and Devlin excused himself.

My mother talked to me for a half hour. She pretty much told me I was coming home over break, though she did say at the last that the final decision was up to me. And though she didn't tell me she was worried about me, it was in her voice.

I did my best to reassure her, then cut the conversation short, before she figured out I was lying.

* * * *

I ended up not coming home over break. I'd been further behind in my science courses than I'd thought I was, and it was all I could do to pass my midterm finals. But I did come home that weekend to Danial's house.

Jenny, my new werecougar stepmother, was there. She hovered over me from the moment I walked in the door, asking me if I wanted her to do some of my laundry, or if I wanted to change and hunt deer in the forest. I asked her about my father, and she said vaguely he was away at meetings most of the time. "But he'll be home for dinner. I'm making some lasagna, and some pie."

I should try to be nice. "Do you need me to help?"

"Sure," she said gratefully. "I'm not much of a cook." She left it at that, but she and I knew what was unsaid: my mother had been a good cook, and a fantastic baker.

A few hours later, my father came home. He smelled me before he had closed the door, and ran into the kitchen to grab me in a big hug. "How are you, Elle?" he said, his blue eyes twinkling, his smile sunny and happy.

Try to be nice. "Good," I said, in a false bright voice. "We've been making dinner."

"Good!" he said, sprawling down in a chair. "Terian and Sun are coming over. And your brother said he'd try to be here, too, but no promises. He's at a late meeting."

It would be great to see Theoron again. I hadn't seen him since Christmas. "Good."

A few minutes later, Terian and Sundown arrived. Sundown came in, and gave me a hug. "I know you aren't related to Sar," she said, giving me a crooked smile. "But I swear you look more like her every time I see you!"

"You should talk," I said, laughing as I hugged her. "You could be her sister!"

"Dinner's ready!" Jenny said from the dining room, her brittle voice cracking a little with forced jovialness.

Sun and I looked at one another meaningfully, and went into the dining room.

We began eating without saying grace. Terian was half demon, so saying grace was kind of out of the question. He'd either have to be in pain, or leave the table.

"This is great!" Theo exclaimed. "Good job, Mate!"

Jenny blushed.

"It's great, Jenny," Terian said appreciatively. "But you've made this before and it tastes better this time. Did you use some different sauce or a new recipe?"

Jenny blushed and looked at me. "I added some spices," I said, wiping my lips with my napkin. "It was bland and needed a little zing."

"Where did you learn of what to add?" my father growled at me, his eyes yellowing just a little.

He knows this is Mom's recipe. "From Cia," I lied innocently. "She said Aran likes this."

Theo nodded, and looked away. Later, he went upstairs with Terian to see to some voicemails, while Jenny, Sun, and I cleared the table.

"You want to take some home?" Jenny asked Sun as she transferred the uneaten lasagna into plastic containers.

"Please!" Sun said, and laughed. "I hate to cook!"

"Me too," Jenny said guiltily. "But someone has to. Theo's away all day, so I kind of have to."

I bit my tongue, wanting to tell Jenny she was spineless if she didn't stand up to my father and tell him how she felt. My mother sure wouldn't have done something all day every day if she hated doing it, at least not without giving everyone an earful.

"Do you need me to help you with the email work?" Sun said, and I cut my eyes over to Jenny in surprise. Last I'd known, my mother was doing all the email work from Devlin's house.

"No, I've got it," Jenny said wearily. "T's not been accepting any new business, as he's overbooked. But he said in May he's going to, so I'll need your help then for sure. I'm just able to do that and cook, and take care of keeping the house neat and the dishes done! There're just not enough hours in the day!"

I bit my lip harder in an effort to keep silent. My mom had had time to do all the email work herself, cook, do a good part of the cleaning and laundry, and have time to spend with me and with my father, not to mention her gardening and other hobbies. What was this lazy woman doing all day that she couldn't keep up?

"I need to get back," Sun said, taking the containers from Jenny. "Sunrise needs to go to bed in a half-hour. Thanks for these!"

"You're welcome!" Jenny called. She turned to me. "Would you like to watch some TV? We have a large one now in the great room."

I was so shocked I went in to make sure she was telling the truth.

She was. *My father would be absolutely appalled.* In one of his dark moods, he'd once told me that television was for those who couldn't read. This room had been his room for reading, and for visiting with friends and family. He would be outraged if he knew a TV was in here—

"We have a Wii, and an Xbox," Jenny said, sitting down and bringing out a stack of games. "I got your father interested in these, and T and Terian often play with us, when they have a free evening." She gave me a smile. "I'm not too bad. But I have to practice a lot."

This is what she did all day. Ugh.

"Want to play something?"

I thought of spending my night here with her playing video games, and I wanted to scream. "No, thanks," I said politely. "I'm exhausted. I'm heading to bed."

I went into my bedroom and shut the door. *Enough being nice.*

I took a shower, and then flopped on the bed. I'd just turned on the TV when I thought I heard shouting. I got out of bed, and listened at the door.

"Lower your voice! Your daughter will hear us!" *Jenny's voice, coming from the great room.*

"She's heard enough spats in her life not to worry," Theo growled. "And I want to know the truth, Jenny. Did Cia ever mention those spices to you?"

"Why do you care?" Jenny was clearly upset. "I thought you liked the food!"

"I did. But I don't like being manipulated. And part of me wonders if Sar asked Elle to do something like that at dinner—"

"You're an ass," Jenny said in a low voice. "Sarelle doesn't care about you, Theo. That should've been obvious to you from her behavior at the wedding! She sure doesn't care what you eat!"

"I wasn't saying she did!" Theo thundered. "I was saying she wanted to get to me!"

"Listen to me right now," Jenny said in that same low voice. "We have had this same fight almost every other night since the wedding. And I'm not having any more, Theo. If you want to spend your days obsessing over Sar, then fine, I'll pack my things and leave. And I'll go west, where I know there are others like us."

"I didn't mean that," Theo said contritely. "I'm just upset, Jen."

"You haven't stopped being upset. You are always like this now. And I can't take being on edge all the time."

"I'm sorry," Theo said softly. "Forgive me, please. I don't mean to make you feel bad."

"But I do feel bad!" Jenny shouted at him. "How can I feel good, when all you and your friends ever do is compare me to Sar? She left you for a vampire, and your worst enemy, Theo! And all I hear is how fucking great she was! Sundown's right, she's a bitch!"

I let out a little gasp. *I thought Sun liked my mother. Does this mean she doesn't really like me, either?*

"She can be," Theo said in a low voice. "But she was Elle's mother when no one else wanted the job. She took care of my child when I couldn't, and when we were attacked in Europe, she shielded Elle's body with her own, even when Elle bit her. And I'll always love her just for that, Jen."

"I didn't know that," Jenny whispered.

I hadn't known that myself. I felt a rush of love for my mother.

"Come downstairs," Theo purred. "And know I want to be with you, not anyone else."

I didn't hear anything after that.

In the morning when I got up I went into the kitchen and saw my brother, Danial's son, T, sitting there, reading the paper. "Hi, Sis," he said affectionately, giving me a hug. "How's college life?"

"Not great," I said, and related the true story of how things had been going.

When I finished, he hugged me again. "What does your therapist say?"

"Rosalyn said that I'd get past it when I was ready. She said not to force it."

"Okay," T said slowly. "Can I help?"

"Not unless you know a spell for happiness."

"If I did, I'd be rich," he said, laughing. "Though it's true that Solutions, Inc. is doing pretty well for itself."

"I was always a little jealous of you," I said softly.

T gave me a shocked look. "Why?"

"Because Dad liked you best, obviously."

"He does not like me best. We aren't speaking right now, in fact."

"That's because he's different now. But he always wanted a son. And you came from Sar and him, T. I'm Theo's daughter, not his or hers."

"You're still his," T said firmly. "I remember how protective he was of you. And he always asks about you, when I go to see him."

"Then why didn't he ever ask me to go into business with him?" I said a little bitterly. "He wanted you to from the moment you were born. He's never asked me to even help out."

"Dad's like that about women," T said with a shrug. "Mom had a lot of trouble convincing him she could do things as well as he could. Dev's kind of the same way."

"Since when are you calling him Dev?" I asked sarcastically.

"I go over once a week and have drinks with him and Lash," T said a little defensively. "He's not a bad guy, Elle."

"Don't try to sell me, T. You know what he did to Mom."

16

"I know Mom forgave him, and if she can, I can," T replied, not blinking. "And Lash'd never hurt any of us, Elle. Theo, on the other hand, is still on my shit list. Luckily we don't have to go to meetings together. He and Terian mostly team up now, and I go with Rip and Brian."

I let out a breath. "T, Dev and Lash asked me to live with them. Mom asked, too."

"So why don't you?"

"Theo'd go apeshit."

"So what? It's your life, Elle. And pretty soon they may have a cub of their own."

I felt engulfed in cold water. "What?"

"Jenny's off the pill," T whispered. "I know because she left a half-used pack in the kitchen garbage last week. Terian was saying some things to Theo that made me guess Theo asked her to." He paused. "He wants another son, Elle. He misses Devon."

I was going to be sick. Devon had been Theo and Sar's werecougar baby. He'd died of SIDS last fall. I'd loved him as much as I loved T.

"I'm sorry, Sis, I didn't think that would upset you," T said, uneasy.

"It's just I miss Devon too," I whispered, brushing at tears. "This makes it seem like they're just going to replace him with another baby."

"Nobody's getting replaced," T said firmly. "I promise you that." He cleared his throat. "I have a few hours. Want to catch an early movie?"

"Sure," I said in relief.

* * * *

The movie was fun, but by the time we returned home, I knew that I wasn't going to feel better until I was either back at school, or moved

17

in with my mom. As much as this house had once been my home, it wasn't anymore. So that afternoon, I got into my little SUV and drove to Hayden.

Lash was at the gate, and he let me in. "Good to see you," he said curiously. "I wasn't told you were coming."

"Is Mom here?"

"She's out shopping with Titus," Lash replied. "But she should be back soon, Elle. Go on in and wait for her."

I drove up to the house, parked, and walked inside.

No one was in the kitchen, and so I went into the living room. I'd just flipped on the TV when my half-sister V sauntered in, dressed to the nines, an arrogant look in her golden eyes.

Now truthfully, T and Devon were also half-siblings. But I'd always just thought of them as brothers. But V, V was always half. And I knew the feeling was mutual.

"Why are you here?" she said in her beautiful voice. "Mom didn't say you were coming."

"It's an unplanned visit," I replied frostily. "Get used to it. I may be living here soon. Your dad asked me to."

"Who's that?" a little girl asked. I saw she was close to V's size, though that didn't tell me much.

"This is Elle, Theo's daughter," V said in a snide tone. "Danial, my uncle, thinks of her as his daughter. But we aren't related really, thank God."

I bit my tongue. Why was my mother never around to hear her?

"She's werecreature by her scent," the other girl said disdainfully. "My father said they are beneath us, good for only guarding their vampire betters."

"That's because your father is an ass," Lash hissed in a low voice, coming up behind her. "And you will not insult either Elle, or any other

18

were in this house, is that understood, Sharon?"

"Yes," Sharon said, cringing back from him a little.

"And you, V," Lash hissed turning to her. "Keep in mind that Sarelle took Elle in as a daughter because she wanted to, out of kindness. But she was forced to have you on Devlin's orders, and she didn't take kindly to it."

V looked stricken, and then anger flooded her face, making her eyes turn red and her fangs elongate. "How dare you speak to me like that?" she hissed at him. "I'm the child of the most powerful Vampire Ruler in the history of the world!"

"He didn't get that rep all on his own," Lash said with a nasty smile. "And he'd scold you himself, child, if he were here."

"I'm going to tell him what you said to me," V said just as nastily. "He'll order you beaten!"

Lash looked at her and burst out laughing. "God, you're foolish. Who do you think would dare beat me?" He crouched down before her. "You think about what you've said to Elle, and to me. And you remember who your father is, and what we are to him. And then you answer me a question: do you want your father to know about your words or not?"

V glared at him, then the redness faded from her eyes, and she dropped her gaze. "No."

"Good choice," Lash hissed. He reached out and hugged her, and after a moment, she hugged him back. "Go upstairs and play, V. Sharon will have to go home soon enough."

V glared over at me, and then she and Sharon ran upstairs.

"She's jealous," a hesitant voice said.

Lash and I looked over to see a young boy peering in from the kitchen. He had two cookies in his hands.

"That she is," Lash hissed softly. "Though God knows she has no reason to be. Sar has never been unfair in her affections." He looked

19

over at me. "Elle, this is Elijah, Sharon's brother. Samuel's son, though you likely guessed that already."

The half-vampire son of the Vampire Ruler of Europe. I held out a hand. "Hi."

"Pleased to meet you," Elijah said, shaking briefly while not letting go of his cookies.

"I need to go shower," Lash said, getting to his feet. "But your mother should be home soon, Elle."

"I should get going," I said. Inwardly I was despondent, as with V here, I'd never want to live here too. And that meant it was back to school.

"Stay…daughter," Lash said a little awkwardly. "Your mother would like to see you, and I want you here, too."

"I'm not your daughter," I said, trying not to sound unkind. "Though it would be easier if I was."

"You're right. If you were my daughter, I'd have spanked V instead of just scolded her," Lash hissed, grinning. "But I meant it about staying."

"I'll come back in a few weekends," I said, getting on my coat. "And please, don't tell my mother anything, okay?"

Lash nodded. "Sure. But call me if you need anything, okay?"

I agreed, and with a last smile, he walked upstairs.

I watched him leave, wondering how he'd gotten to be on such bad terms with my father. *He seems like such a do right guy.*

I felt a tug on my hand and looked down. Elijah was holding my hand. "Where do you live?" he said.

"I'm at school. College."

"What's it called?"

"Penn State."

"Is it big?"

"Pretty big."

"Can I come and visit?"

"Your father wouldn't like that," I said, laughing a little. "Your father doesn't like me."

"I like you," he said shyly. "May I visit you?"

"Sure," I said, going to the door. "But you'd better bring guards, Elijah. It's a big world out there."

"Ok," I heard him say before the door shut behind me.

* * * *

I went back to school, and lost myself in work. A month later, I was in the food court when a guy sat down at my table.

I gave him a cold look, and said in my mom's best nasty voice, "Are you lost?"

"No," he said, giving me a heart-melting smile. "I've found you."

I rolled my eyes. "Look, I don't know you."

"You do, you just don't recognize me," he said, giving me a wide grin.

I looked him over skeptically. He was cute, if a little young looking. *Must be a freshman.* He was medium size, his skin tanned, and his brown hair cut in a neat style, almost military. His eyes were hazel colored, and seemed friendly. And his body...his body was very nice. For his youth, he looked very fit and muscular. "I don't."

"It's Elijah," he said, grinning wider. "I got older, Elle."

I gaped at him. "I saw you a month ago. You were five!"

"I'm aging fast," he admitted, uneasy. "My father's worried about it, though he acts like everything's okay. But there's a good point, as I'll soon be old enough to look like I belong here."

"How old are you, really?"

"Three months," he said, coloring slightly. "I learn fast, but nothing in a book tells you how not to be embarrassed about something so abnormal about yourself."

"Don't be embarrassed," I said quickly. "I aged fast, too, because I stayed in animal form for months when I was young. It was hard to cope with, looking so much older than I was."

"Oh look, it's the virgin princess!" a passing boy said sarcastically. "Don't waste your time, pal. She's frigid as a metal post in January."

Elijah looked at the boy, his eyes flashed vampiric red, and then he got to his feet. "You will apologize to her, now, cretin," he growled. "And then I'm taking you outside to thrash you."

"I'm not apologizing!" the boy called back, still walking. "But you can come outside if you want to!"

Elijah strode after him. I grabbed my stuff as fast as I could and followed. By the time I got outside, Elijah was holding the boy by the scruff of his neck and the boy was pleading for mercy.

"Apologize!" Elijah hissed, his fangs elongating slightly.

"I apologize!" the boy yelped.

Elijah shoved him, and he went sprawling.

I heard the squeal of police sirens, and grabbed hold of Elijah. "In here!"

We ducked into the library, and hid in the book stacks. "Why are we hiding?" Elijah asked.

"Shh!" I said. "You have to be quiet. We're hiding because you can't beat a student up on campus without being arrested."

"But he was being ungentlemanly. And I didn't actually beat him."

"Doesn't matter."

"How uncivilized," Elijah mused.

"Young Master, we must go home," a rumbling voice said. "Your father will be searching for you. I do not want to be disciplined." A large man appeared suddenly behind us, looking stern.

"Sure," Elijah said, turning to me. "But mark this spot, Harp. I'll want to come back here and see this woman when we next have an opportunity."

"She is a comely one," Harp said, his red eyes flicking over me. "It is done, young Master. We can return here at your will."

"Is this your demon?" I asked politely.

"Yes. Both my sister and I have one. They are with us at almost all times."

And I thought my father had been overprotective! *Geez.*

"Goodbye," Elijah said seriously. "I hope to see you soon, Elle."

"Sure," I said, smiling. "Though it's going to be May soon. I'll be out of school."

"Call me, if you are going to be at Hayden," Elijah said, handing me a slip of paper. "This is my cell."

Shit! Give him your number too! I tore off part of the paper, and wrote down my cell in tiny numbers. "Here is mine."

"Thanks," Elijah said, taking it. "Please be careful. You are here without any guards."

"I can take care of myself," I said proudly.

"I want to take care of you," Elijah said seriously. Then he reached out and brushed my cheek gently, moving a strand of hair away from my face.

Part of me knew he was just young, probably copying something from a movie he'd seen. But no one had ever said anything like that to me before. Before I knew it, I kissed him. Though he was clearly shocked, before long he kissed me back.

"Break it up," Harp rumbled, pushing us gently apart. "This is a library, children, not a barn. And we must be home."

"Call me, please," Elijah encouraged, and then they disappeared.

Chapter Two

That next week was wonderful. I spoke to Elijah every night for hours. He texted to me some days, as well. Every weekend, he managed to come and visit for a few hours.

We'd take walks outside, get pizza, and see movies, and sometimes just make out in my room. I didn't seem to worry about being alone with him. He also didn't push things to the next level.

As before, my coursework slid a little, but I didn't care. It was almost the end of the semester, anyway.

Finally, finals were over, and I was heading home, elated that I could enjoy my first real vacation in months with my new boyfriend. But when I got there, I found that Hayden had been attacked, my mother and Lash were missing, and Danial was presumed alive but captured. And Devlin's demon, Titus, was in Hell.

I cried for a while in my Mom's sewing room, as Devlin talked strategy with Leri, Titus's witch lover. That night, they got Titus out of hell.

Better than that, my dad Danial also came in about midnight, alive and unhurt. I wrapped my arms around him before he could say anything. "Where have you been? I was so worried, Dad!"

"Hiding," he said angrily. "Those bastards wanted to obliterate us."

"Have they found…um, Lady?"

"She's safe with Lash at Michael's hotel on the coast. Don't worry, Elle. Everything's going to be fine."

I hugged my dad, hoping he was right.

Instead, everything went right to shit. Danial came to me two days later to say my mother had been kidnapped with Lash. Michael had them. He also told me I was not to leave Hayden under pain of death, as attacks had happened to vampires all over the world.

I tried Elijah on his cell, but got no answer. I left several messages, but he didn't call me back.

Devlin tortured some of the prisoners captured during the attack that night. Danial helped him. I could hear them shouting angrily in the basement, and cries of pain. I didn't feel sorry for the human men and women, even though I knew my father wasn't asking them any questions, he was just making them scream. He was doing it for the same reason Devlin was: they couldn't touch Michael, and even though Lash was with her, it was a safe bet that what had happened once to my mother and me was happening to her again. And for all their promises and power and immortality, they were powerless to stop it.

* * * *

Two days later, I was in my mother's book room, reading one of her suspense novels when I heard Kyle, Lash's second-in-command, come in with some children. I was amazed to find out they were the children and grandchildren of the man who'd masterminded the attack that had led to my mother being kidnapped. Caitlyn got them into one of the guest rooms, and settled them in with blankets, and sleeping bags, while Kyle filled me in on who they were.

I wasn't surprised to find that Devlin himself had gone after the man, and brought him back to Hayden the night before. According to Kyle, that man, Peter, was now a vampire too. "I couldn't kill children," Kyle said in a low tone. "I know Lash could've—"

I felt my stomach twist. That couldn't be true, it couldn't.

"—but this way, no one dies. Hopefully, it will make an ally out of an enemy."

"Any word from my mom or Lash?"

Kyle shook his head. "Devlin is almost berserk with grief. He's in his room, with Titus standing guard."

"What's going to happen?"

"I don't know," he said wearily. "I need Lash here to help me plan. We have nothing to go on and no idea where they are. Some attacks are still taking place."

"What about Samuel? Do we know what happened to him and his family?"

"Harriet was killed. But Samuel escaped, as did the children."

I breathed a sigh of relief. "Where are they? Elijah doesn't answer his cell."

Kyle gave me a look and tilted his head. "I didn't know you knew him."

I blushed, and Kyle said, "Ah." He gave me a knowing look. "He's safe, but Samuel is being very careful. One of his guards betrayed him, and if it weren't for those demons, the children would both be dead."

"I have to talk to him," I said urgently. "Can you find out how?"

"I'll try," he said, nodding. "But it'll take a while."

I nodded.

* * * *

That week passed like individual sands falling one by one through an hourglass. And each one cut me, as I waited to hear some word about Elijah.

Finally, on Friday, Kyle came to me and gave me a slip of paper. "That's a number to reach Samuel. Sorry, it's the best I could do."

I nodded, and said, "Thanks."

A minute later I was dialing.

"Hello?" a cautious voice said.

"Hi. Is Elijah there?"

"Who is this?"

I swallowed. "Elle. Danial's daughter."

There was silence, and it went on and on.

"Hello?" I said again, finally. "Is anyone there?"

"My son has talked to me about you," Samuel said in a grating tone. "I can see he cares for you. I need to ask if you care for him, if you have been honest in your words to him."

What had Elijah said about me to his father? "Yes, I have."

"I want you to know I disapprove of you two being together," Samuel said, aloof. "But in the end, it's his choice, Elle."

I wanted to tell him he was a jackass, but couldn't seem to get the words out.

"You are invited here to visit him, as he badly wants to see you. I believe V is coming tomorrow. You may come with her, if you choose."

"That would be good. Thank you."

"Goodbye then." Click.

God, he's a jerk. I put down my cell, and went in search of V. I found her in her room, listening to music. I snapped it off, and she turned to look at me, scowling. "What's your problem?"

"Why didn't you tell me that you were seeing Sharon tomorrow?"

"Why would I?" V said nastily. "You aren't her friend."

"I'm Elijah's friend," I said proudly. "In fact, we're more than friends. So I'll be going with you."

"Sure," V said with a sultry smile. "I'm leaving about two. Meet me at the base of the stairs."

I nodded, and walked out, even as V called after me to put her music back on.

* * * *

I was at the stairs at quarter of two. But when it was five after, I went in search of V. At two-thirty, I finally called Titus. "V left at noon with Rip," he rumbled apologetically. "We did not know you were supposed to go, too, Elle."

My fury was white hot by then. "Can you take me there now?"

"Sure," Titus rumbled, and a few moments later, we were in Europe.

I looked around. It was a bright sunny day, and the air was a little cold. I was in some kind of garden.

A second later, Harp appeared. "Titus," he said in greeting. "Ah, Elle. Have you come to see Elijah?"

"Yes."

"Call my cell when you wish to go home," Titus rumbled, and disappeared.

"Come," Harp said pleasantly. "Elijah is in the study, or he was a moment ago."

I followed him inside, and we walked up a flight of stairs. I was glad not to see Samuel.

"I'm not supposed to leave him alone for a moment," Harp said with a sigh. "But I have needs, too. Lucky for me the kitchen maid likes demon meat."

It took me a moment to understand what he'd said, and I flushed. By then we were at a door. "Go on in," he said. "Yell if you need something." Then he walked out.

I turned to the door, grasped the handle, and opened it. It took my eyes a moment to adjust to the gloom. When they did I gasped. Elijah was there all right. And V was with him. He was in a chair, moaning loudly. Her head was bobbing in his lap, as she deep-throated him.

Before I could gather my wits, Elijah gasped, jerking, and grabbed

V by her hair, holding her to him. She struggled a little, and then he released her, gasping still. She let the still hard length of him slide out of her mouth and then kissed the still-quivering tip of him. "There," she said in a satisfied voice. "Told you I'd make you feel better."

"God, it was so good, V!" Elijah panted. "I loved it. I love you!"

I ran from the room, directly into Harp. When I demanded he take me home at once, he did.

We arrived at Hayden's gates. "I'm sorry, I can't teleport inside," he said. "You'll have to call Titus."

I wasn't calling anyone! Who gave a flying fuck if it was pouring? "Thanks!"

I strode inside and stalked up the long drive, the scene playing over and over in my head again and again: V sucking him, and Elijah coming, telling her he loved her. By the time I'd reached the main door I was crying, and soaked from the rainstorm.

God, how can he have done that? Venus is so young! Then I remembered her apparent skill, and how young Elijah truly was. God, what if she'd seduced him when he was only a child? I felt sick as I approached the front door, and knocked.

Seth let me in, and handed me a towel. "Your father told me to let you know he is with his donors tonight. But he'll be available after ten, if you should need him."

Thanks a lot. "Okay."

I walked inside. I didn't want to face V, or hear her sarcastic and triumphant comments. I also didn't want to go to bed, so I could play the scene a few more times in my head. Instead, I walked to the ballroom, following the sound of music. Devlin was there, playing the "Moonlight Sonata." I stood at the door and let the music wash over me. It made me feel better; it was so despondent and beautiful.

When it ended, Devlin began again. Then a third time.

I walked closer to him, until I was behind him, but not within

30

reach, lest I startle him. "It's beautiful," I said softly.

"Sar loved this piece," Devlin whispered, not missing a note. "She always asked me to play it for her. I think if I play it enough, perhaps she'll appear."

I looked at his hands. They were red, and raw, though not bleeding. But it was proof he'd been playing for hours. "Stop," I said gently.

Devlin acted as if he did not hear me.

I sat down beside him, and grabbed his hands. "Stop!"

Devlin gave a ragged breath. "Okay."

"Why don't you go to bed?" I said, feeling awkward to be attempting to care for him, this man who I didn't like at all. "You need rest."

"I cannot rest," he said, swaying a little. "My dreams are filled with her crying out to me to save her, and I fail over and over! I can't bear it, Elle! I'm going mad!"

I let out a breath. "She wouldn't want you to do this, Devlin. She would want you to be strong, to be thinking of some way to get to her, to save her from Michael."

"It's too late," Devlin whispered brokenly. "Michael has told me she is pregnant, and it's his." He put his head in his hands. "He hurt her, and I didn't stop him. What the hell good am I? What if I never see her again? And even if he does let her come back to me, how can I ever ask her to be mine again knowing I couldn't fucking protect her?"

The last he screamed, and then he was sobbing. Though I'd disliked him so long, I grabbed hold of him, and hugged him. He burrowed into me, his arms going around me as he crushed me to him. Still he sobbed, his tears soaking my shirt.

"Shh," I whispered gently. "Shh."

After a few minutes, Devlin gave a last ragged breath, and swallowed. "I apologize," he said in his rich voice. "You have lost your mother. It should be you doing the crying, and me doing the comforting."

"Mom raised me to be tough," I said, cracking a smile. "And I'm not a child anymore, Devlin."

Devlin gave me an up and down look. "So you are not."

I blushed faintly, and he smiled. "Or perhaps you are, to blush over such an innocuous observation."

"Nothing you have ever said in your life was innocuous," I said sarcastically.

"Tell me you've not had better compliments, Elle, than to be noted for being a woman and not a girl."

I thought of Elijah, and swallowed hard. "Not lately."

Devlin looked at me sideways. "What is wrong?"

"I had someone I thought cared for me," I said hesitantly. "And I found him with someone else. I'm still shocked that he could do that to me, after how he said he felt about me."

"Men do stupid things," Devlin said in a comforting tone. "If you care for him, forgive him."

"He didn't even see me walk in on them."

Devlin looked appalled, and then blushed faintly. "Sometimes men are…involved in what they are doing. And it takes a moment to notice someone watching."

I glared at him, exasperated. "What kind of answer is that? Would you just forgive my mother, if she was with someone else, and you found them together? And I mean someone she wanted to be with."

"I forgave her for Lash," Devlin said, after a moment. "I knew even back then that it wasn't really for me that she'd saved him, it was because she loved him. So, yes. If you love someone, really love them, you forgive them most anything."

"I can't forgive him," I said a little tearfully. "Does that mean I didn't really love him? God…!"

"Shh," Devlin said, putting his arms around me. "If he shows remorse, think about forgiving him. If he does not...then tell me his name and I'll torture him a little, as any good uncle would do."

I snorted, still trying not to cry. God, it felt so good to be held, to have someone tell me it was going to be all right. I nestled into his throat, and he hugged me tighter, rocking me a little. Then he began to sing to me.

I realized with shock it was a version of "Silent Lucidity". I went limp in his arms, letting his voice wash over me. I'd heard Devlin sing to Mom once, in the kitchen at Danial's house. But this was different. This time, that rich and smooth voice was all meant for me, every delicious clear crystal note.

When he finished, I looked up at him, and he gave me a questioning look, and then I abruptly kissed him, grabbing his face in my hands.

A tremor went through him, and then he was almost crushing me, pulling me against his body as his lips devoured mine. He turned and in a smooth motion pulled me astride him. I went rigid as I felt the hardness of his erection forming between my legs.

Devlin growled a little, and began running his fangs over my neck, licking me and biting me gently. I let out a moan, feeling the brush of his fangs in his skillful kisses.

He slid his left hand down from around my shoulders and cupped my breast, squeezing it gently.

I swayed a little in his arms, lost in sensation. God, Elijah had never felt like this! *And there's some scent rising up from him that smells so sweet, almost like cherry trees...*

Devlin was shaking now, and his hips were thrusting gently against mine, pressing that steel rod of his to me. He let out a primal, guttural sound of pure need, and I went utterly still in fear, freezing up in his arms.

Devlin felt it and pulled back to look at me, his eyes tinged red, and his fangs bared as he panted. Then he shut his eyes tight, and shook his head. "No, we can't do this," he whispered. "I can't do this."

I didn't move. I was afraid to.

"I apologize for my behavior," he said raggedly. "I have not been with anyone since your mother. I'm…overwrought." He took a breath. "Please get up, Elle."

Part of me knew it was wrong to not get off him right then. But the other part had been wanting release for months, it just hadn't trusted any of the men I knew to give me that release. That part of me was telling me loudly not to get up off of him. It was telling me that this was a man I could trust to give me what I needed in spades. I kissed him passionately again, plunging my tongue into his mouth.

The effect was instantaneous. Devlin shuddered and kissed me back again, sliding down off the piano bench with me still astride him. And then he was on top of me on the floor, his legs between my spread ones.

He was kissing me hungrily, his hands roaming my body, and I felt all of my longing to mate, my longing for a man to rise up in me the way it hadn't since being with Hans years ago. And I just didn't care if what we were doing was wrong, because God damn it, I was tired of always trying to do everything right!

"No," he said suddenly, pushing up from me. "God damn it, Elle, we can't do this!"

"Please," I breathed, shaking a little. "Please don't stop. I want you to touch me."

Devlin shut his red eyes, and gritted his fangs. "Not as much as I want to. If you were anyone else, I'd be in you already, girl. But you're my niece, and my Oathed One's daughter. I may be a bastard, but I'm not a complete one."

"We aren't related by blood, not at all," I said, trying to convince him. I reached up to run my hands up under his shirt and he moaned softly, feeling me stroke his chest. "I'm just a woman who wants to be loved. And you're just a man who needs release—" I said the last as I reached down into his pants and ran my hand over his erect penis, squeezing the tip which was almost poking out near his belt.

Devlin closed his eyes and moaned, baring his fangs wide as he swayed above me. I took the opportunity to quickly slide down my jeans. I pulled down his zipper, reached in and grabbed hold of his hard dick again, as I moved into position beneath him.

Devlin suddenly grabbed my wrists so hard I yelped in pain. "STOP IT!" he shouted, his eyes solid red.

I shivered in fear beneath him, afraid to speak.

"Say I did fuck you right here on this floor! What about after? What am I supposed to tell your mother, Elle? What are you going to tell Danial?"

"I don't have to tell them anything!" I yelled.

"I do," he said, zipping his pants up, and easing back off me. "No matter how good it would feel, Elle…it would never go away, once it was done. We'd always remember, and it would be something you always regretted, just as I would. Put your clothes on."

I tried to gather back some of my pieces of pride along with the scattered bits of clothing. "You're a legend, like Don Juan," I whispered, putting on my jeans. "Why would I regret it?"

"Because I don't love you, and you know that. I love your mother. I'm your uncle; no matter we don't share blood. And I can't be that person and still be your lover, and not have any decency." He rolled his red-tinted eyes. "And I'm a father now, besides. I cannot act like a man who has no boundaries; do you understand? I'm not free anymore to indulge my desires without a thought to the consequences!"

"I'm sorry," I whispered. "I…I haven't been with anyone since I was attacked."

"You're a young werecougar so it's normal to want sex," Devlin said, getting to his feet. "I am sorry, but I don't think you should leave the grounds right now, it's too dangerous. But there are many men here, Elle. All of them would leap at the chance to bed you, if you but told them you wanted them, and I told them it was permitted. So if you like—"

"No. I don't want to do that."

"Then why do you want me?" Devlin said, still keeping his distance from me. "You've tried to grab me before, Elle, this isn't the first time."

I blushed. "I'm aware of that."

"I've never encouraged you to act as anything other than my niece, never! And you have acted as though you disliked me for most of your life; save those times you've tried to seduce me. Do you want me because you're in love with me? And if not, then what is your reason for acting this way?"

I felt heat suffuse my face. "No. The first time when you were teaching me piano...I did it because I thought you'd say yes, because of how Danial always talked about you wanting sex."

Devlin rolled his eyes, and let out a breath. "Not with my niece."

"But this time, I made advances because I trust you, Devlin. Next to my father, you're the only man I trust. So if we were together...I know I'd be safe. It would be good; it wouldn't...wouldn't be..."

Devlin sighed, and there was a lot of longing in that sound. "No one will hurt you, Elle, I promise. Pick one of my men, and tell me his name. It will be easy for me to arrange."

All his guards were werebear. And it had been a werebear who had raped me. "I can't." I said brokenly. "They're all bears. I don't want...a bear."

"I understand that you might not," he said in a low voice. "But they would not—"

"I can't ever be with a bear," I said more forcefully. "Just scenting them sometimes is too much."

"Kyle is not werebear," he said quietly. "Do you find him attractive?"

"No," I said honestly. "He's very nice. But I couldn't think of him as more than a guard, not ever." *God, let him not suggest Rip next!*

Devlin swore in some other language. "Go to bed, niece. I'll speak to Leri tonight. She'll come to you later on with some solution to your desires that doesn't compromise either of us."

I nodded, and fled to my room.

Chapter Three

A few hours later, Leri arrived at my bedroom door. She was in a long black velvet panne' dress, her long brown hair unbound.

"How old are you?" I said suddenly, before she could speak.

"About twenty-two," she said, laughing. "At least appearance-wise. That's all I'm admitting to."

I laughed too, and then she came over and sat on my bed, patting it. "Sit down, Elle. Devlin came to see me, as he told you he would. And I have something for you to drink, if you want it."

"What is it?"

"Many are feeling tension, with the human children being here, and hunters outside our walls. They do not dare to leave Hayden, not even to slack their various appetites. Most of that, I'm afraid, is because Lash is not here at his post, as he has been for decades. The bears are good guards, but he's in a league all his own. All good soldiers worry when their trusted general is absent from the battlefield."

"I'm worried about him and my mom."

"Lash will take care of her," Leri said flatly. "That's his job, Elle. She'll be back before long. Titus is working hard to find them both."

"But—"

"Drop it," Leri said in a biting tone. "You can do nothing. Speaking of this will not only make you upset, but ruin your dreams. And you need good ones, according to Devlin."

What? I gave her a look.

"I was instructed to give you a potion to encourage dreams. To invite into your dreams a male of your choosing." She handed me a small vial. "You do not have to tell me who it will be. But it would be best if you told me who you wanted to dream of. And be honest, because if you tell me one man's name, and fantasize about another man, the dream could become a nightmare that would be real enough to cause your death." She grimaced at me. "Dreams are nothing to play with, child. But Devlin is my master, and I obey his commands, even ones I doubt the wisdom of."

Dare I tell her the truth? What if I have a nightmare because I don't? "I'm embarrassed."

"You should not be embarrassed to speak about your desire for sex. It is not only normal, but also a central part of a healthy mind. Now who is it?"

"Devlin," I said, blushing furiously. "I've fantasized about him many times, even though as a person I don't really like him. I don't even know why. But tonight, earlier, I kind of …well, I…"

"Say no more," Leri said bluntly. "He smelled so strongly of unfulfilled desire when he came to see me that I guessed what almost happened between you two." She smiled a pirate's grin. "Most every woman that's ever met Devlin fantasized about him at some time. It's nothing to be ashamed of."

"Can you really do it, let me dream of him? Him, how he would really be, with a woman he desired?"

"I can," Leri said seductively. "But are you sure you want that, to have him in your dreams? He's not a boy, Elle; he's a four-hundred-year old vampire. His mind is powerful: he's easily going to take control of your dreams from you as soon as they begin, and then they'll be under his control for the rest of the night. You know what kind of a man he is. Do you want to know what a man like him dreams of doing to women? Do you want to dream that dream with him over and over? Because he'll sleep until dusk tomorrow. As long as he dreams, he will be in control and you will not be able to wake. And in the mood he was in tonight, his dreams will be as wet, dark, and deep as an ocean's black fathomless trench."

I shivered. "Yes, on the condition that the dream does not involve anyone else I know besides him. I couldn't deal with Danial showing up, or my mom, or Lash—"

"No one but him, and others you wouldn't know," Leri said, nodding. "That can probably be arranged, with an additional spell, though he may fight me a tad. You're sure you want this?"

I nodded.

"Then what will you give me, in return for letting you have your desire?" Leri said slyly. "What you're asking is not something Devlin would agree to. If he found out I did this, he would be furious, though I don't see any harm, especially as I'll make sure he believes it to be just a dream." She grinned.

"What do you want from me?"

"I know you have babysat for Sundown before, Elle. Offer to do so again. And when you do, call me, in order that I might bring my granddaughter Sunrise here to visit for a few hours."

This sounded sinister. "Why?"

"Because they do not let me see her, not ever, and I want to spend time with her, faerie mother to faerie child. Titus would like it, too. You do this for me a few times, and I'll consider the debt paid in full."

"Agreed." Screw Sundown, she probably thought I was a bitch, all the while telling me she was my friend. And it wouldn't hurt anything.

"Be warned again, this is not your fantasy, it will be his. Dev is known for his odd lusts. I know of what happened to you. I want you to be prepared that you may find yourself in a similar position with him in his dreams, if not worse. Can you handle that? Are you sure you even want to?"

"Yes," I said, nodding. "Please, let's get started, before I lose my nerve."

"Very well," she said. "Take this, and think of him. He's already asleep, as I gave him a sleeping potion at his request. And remember, no matter how your dream turns out, I expect you to honor your promise to me."

I nodded, took the potion, and downed it before I could talk myself out of it.

Leri took back the empty vial. "I'll say it again: only he can stop the dream. You'll be with him until it ends for him, whenever that is. So whatever happens, keep breathing."

She left, shutting the door behind her.

I snuggled down into bed, and promptly fell asleep.

When I opened my eyes, I was in another room. I looked around in wonder. This looked like a castle, with stone, and it was cold, so cold!

The door opened with a creak. An older man came in, with a young man following. My mouth dropped open when I saw they both had light golden eyes. "There she is, my son," the elder man said in a rich voice. It was almost Devlin's voice, but rougher somehow. "She's a virgin, so you must be careful."

"I don't want to be careful," the young man said lustily, and my eyes widened to see that it was Devlin, but not as I knew him. This Devlin was much younger, barely more than a boy, and by the ruddy flush of his skin, he was human.

"You will control yourself!" the man said, cuffing Devlin upside his head. "Women are enjoyed best when they are both wet and willing. As I've told you, it is a well-known fact that in order for conception, a woman must enjoy the act. I intend for you to make me a grandfather someday soon, Dev. And not just legitimately, either. Our attributes are too perfect for us not to spread them like seeds in the fertile fields around us. Now, get on the bed and take her. If we're lucky, you'll have your first bastard son in nine-months' time."

Devlin cast an angry look at his father, and then stepped closer to me, taking off his clothes. I saw when he was naked that he was just as large as I'd always thought him to be and that though his body was much more muscular, it was also not so filled out as he appeared later in his life. *He has to be what, sixteen, seventeen?*

He came closer to me, and I backed up a little on the bed.

"Seduce her, as you have seen me demonstrate," his father said, pulling up a chair beside the bed. "Act like a man, not an animal."

Devlin began to kiss me, and before long I was moaning into his mouth, our tongues entangled. When he pressed me back, I parted my legs for him, and he slipped between them. Then he was deftly pushing up my dress, and laying his hips carefully over mine.

I felt the press of him, but he was so large he couldn't enter me. He let out a frustrated sound. "I can't get inside, Father. She's too small."

"Stroke her gently," his father said. "She will open her petals to you as a flower does."

Devlin rubbed the tip of himself on my soft opening, and I moaned, parting my legs a little further. He slipped the head of himself inside, and then pulled out, and rubbed again. He did this over and over, until I was slippery with my desire for him.

He pushed in with a moan, and then I felt him hit something within me. "I cannot get farther," he panted. "Something bars the way."

"It is her maidenhead. A good fast thrust will break it." His father's voice was weighty with lust now.

Devlin reached under my hips, and then he pushed hard, sliding into me with a loud cry of triumph. I let out a scream as I felt him tear me.

"Do not move, Dev!" his father said sharply. "You are large, and she needs time to adjust to you. Kiss her, until you feel some of the pressure on your organ diminish."

Devlin was trembling, but he kissed me, and I responded. Soon after he began moving, his breaths coming fast as he stroked me.

"Women must come first if they are to come at all," his father said sternly. "Always remember that! It will be easy for you to give a woman pleasure, just as it is for me. Just stroke her a little, and the stimulation of your body moving inside hers should be enough. You will feel her body contract around yours when she orgasms. It is one of the best sensations a man can feel, so make sure to relish it!"

Devlin stroked me faster, panting, and sure enough, I felt the orgasm slide over me like a wave, and I embraced it, letting out cry after cry of pleasure as I pushed my body as close as I could to his.

Devlin was wild now, and he drove into me deeply, causing me some pain. And then he was jerking on me, shouting as he spent himself in me.

He pulled back from me, his golden eyes a little scared. "Did I hurt you?" he asked almost formally.

"No," I said gently.

"What is your name?"

"Matilda." I heard the words from my lips, and realized I had no control over what I was saying. Devlin indeed had control of the dream.

"Thank you, Matilda," he said formally, withdrawing from me. At once, the dream dissolved to be replaced by another.

In this one, Devlin was older, but still human. He was some kind of guard by his dress and the sword at his belt, and I was a serving wench. He took me over his father's banquet table, again making me scream with pleasure.

The dream changed again. Now I was in a bedroom, and Devlin was coming toward me, his golden eyes luminous. But when he touched me, his skin was like ice, and I knew he was vampire. This time, when he had me, he bit me, his fangs intensifying my orgasm to the point I thought I was dying. When I began to drift as he climaxed, he looked down at me with his fangs bared, his face covered in my blood, and then the dream changed again.

Again I was in a bedroom, wearing a robe. Again Devlin came in, and had sex with me. But this time he not only bit me, he gave me his blood. And when he asked me after to stand, I felt fangs in my mouth, and he shushed me, before I could talk.

"Your lover waits for you, Catherine," he said gently. "And your Oathing ceremony will be in a few hours. You need to practice talking, or you will not be able to speak the words of your Oath to your intended."

"I love you," I whispered awkwardly, cutting my lips on my sharp teeth. "Please, I—"

"That will pass," he said a little coldly. "Now come."

The dream dissolved again, and now I was in a black robe, lying before a fire.

Devlin came in and looked at me with eyes that were like pools of fire.

"No," I said in fear, backing away on my hands and knees.

"Yes, Sar," he said, desire pouring through his voice. He took a step toward me, and then the dream fragmented, and I felt Devlin growling in my ear.

"Anna," he whispered in longing. "Anna!"

I turned to him and smiled, and he looked at me with such love and joy, I think I almost fell in love with him. When he kissed me it was the gentlest, most loving kiss of my life. Then he began to touch me, whispering that he loved me, that I was everything to him, and I went limp in his arms from sheer wanting. For the first time he made love to me gently with emotion, and I heard him sing to me in his beautiful unearthly voice. He told me as he came that he loved me, that he would always love me, that my blood was the sweetest in the world, and that he was mine. And I told him I loved him too as he lay panting in my arms, and he sighed so happily as he snuggled against me.

Lying there, I decided that I understood completely now why my mother had decided to be with him, why she stayed with him after all he'd done to her. I had never felt so loved, so cherished, so utterly content as he had just made me feel. I had read about romance and sex, and fantasized about men, and how good it could be. And being with him like this was so far beyond my fantasies, so much more magical than anything I'd ever imagined. I looked down at him in my arms, and wanted to tell him that he was everything, that being without him was unimaginable, that it had been completely fulfilling in every way that counted. But I could say nothing.

Then that dream dissolved into blackness.

I opened my eyes to find him before me, playing the piano in the ballroom as he had earlier in the evening. When he turned to me, I saw his desire for me. To my shock this time, I was not another woman he'd once known, I was myself.

"Niece," he said in a seductive voice. "Come closer."

I came to him, and he hugged me. Then he kissed me hungrily, and I kissed him back. As before, he pulled me onto his lap, straddling me. But this time he pushed my hips down on him.

"Feel me, Elle?" he whispered. "You've got me so hard I'm throbbing."

"I feel it," I moaned. "I want you to take me. I've wanted you inside me for years!" I was appalled at the words coming out of my mouth, and I couldn't stop them!

"I've wanted to be inside you for years," he murmured throatily. "From the first time I scented you were becoming woman, seeing your breasts fill out, and your hips becoming so curvaceous and inviting, I've thought about it!"

I ripped open his shirt, and took his nipple in my mouth, sucking gently. Devlin let out a cry, and cupped my head to his chest as I sucked harder.

"So you want to suck on me, do you?" he said with a leer. "I have something better to fill your mouth, Niece."

"Please," I said, going to my knees. "I want your hard cock in my mouth. I want to hear you come!"

Shit! How can I be saying this? I didn't want to be so…so sluttish! *I want to be loved!*

Devlin let out a shuddering breath, and I undid his pants, sliding them down. His penis was purple with blood, and quivering slightly, already leaking semen.

I licked the tip of it, and sucked gently, and he convulsed, grabbing hold of my shoulders. Then I teased him with my tongue, sliding it down the shaft of him as I massaged the head of him with my lips.

Devlin was panting now, the breaths tearing out of him. When I slid the entire length of him inside my mouth and throat, he let out a scream. I moved on him fast, sucking gently, making my mouth as tight as I could.

"God, you're so warm and tight!" he groaned. "God, it feels so good!"

I bit him gently without missing a stroke, and when he felt my teeth on him he screamed, and I felt him spurt, his seed spilling into my throat in a river as he arched his back, trying to get himself as deep as he could into me. But his manhood was already as deep in my throat as possible, and so I just swallowed over and over fast, massaging his balls in my hands.

Devlin screamed so loud he shattered the bulbs above us, and we were plunged into darkness. But that didn't matter, as my night vision was cougar, and I could see him easily.

I felt the tension leave him as he finished, and then I slid him out of my mouth, kissing him gently.

"God, you were perfect," he groaned, "That was the best oral sex of my life!"

"Thank you, uncle," I said sexily. "Do you want more?"

"Yes, later," he said eagerly, zipping his pants. "But come with me. There are better places to pleasure ourselves than a hard floor."

He extended his hand, and I took it. He led me naked upstairs to his room, and sat me down, then stood before me.

"I want someone to join us," he said. "Name your man."

"Seth," I said quickly. He dialed his cell, and a moment later, he let Seth into the room.

Seth looked at me sitting there naked, and then at Devlin. "This is okay?"

Devlin nodded. "But first, she needs an orgasm, Seth. Can you do that without penetrating her?"

"Yes," Seth said eagerly. He knelt before me, parting my legs, and I felt his mouth on my clit, stroking me with his tongue. Devlin lay next to me, kissing me, and running his fangs over my throat.

I was so afraid, knowing Seth was bear, smelling that musky oily scent, and yet, I wanted to come badly. A few moments later, I climaxed screaming, and Devlin bit down into my neck, intensifying the orgasm. I convulsed hard, feeling him swallowing me down, his mouth latched onto my throat as Seth's was latched to my groin.

Seth withdrew his tongue from me, as I gave a few last gasps. "Can I have her now?"

"Yes, but change form," Devlin said in a dark voice. "Have her as bear."

"No!" I said, but Devlin had hold of me, and he held me where I was, even as I struggled.

Seth let out a growl. He had become a huge bear, his black fur thick and shaggy. He put his paws on the bed on either side of me, as Devlin turned me over so I was on my stomach.

"Please, don't!" I screamed. "Please!" I tried to change to cougar, but I couldn't!

I felt Seth's fangs gently grip the back of my neck to hold me still, and I froze. Next, I felt Seth's fur brushing my naked skin, then the weight of his massive body, and then his massive organ slid into me,

47

and I let out a whimper, even as I began crying. And then he was growling softly as he thrust into me, and I was panting, my fear so strong, but my body betraying me as I responded to him. Because Seth wasn't being rough, he was being gentle, as no true animal would be. I tried hard to shut off the animal side of myself feeling panic, to just experience this through my human side feeling pleasure.

"That's it," Devlin purred. "Seth won't hurt you, Elle. He is not an animal, merely a man in the form of one. Relax and let the pleasure fill you." He kissed me all over my face, his hand on my cheeks. "You're safe. Say it, Elle."

"I'm safe," I rasped out, as Seth pushed himself deeply inside me over and over.

"Again," he whispered. "Once more for me."

"I'm safe," I said again. With that, I felt the first stirrings of an orgasm run over me. I let out a gasp of pleasure.

Devlin responded instantly; he plunged his tongue into my mouth, and I tried to eat him, I was so filled with desire. He put my hand on his manhood that was so engorged it seemed to be a club. He slid my hand down the length of him as I moaned, and then back up, and then I went wild, taking him again in my mouth and he screamed, thrusting into me so hard he hurt me, his movements as frantic now as Seth's were. They both came shouting, and I came too, biting down on Devlin's penis so hard I drew blood. He shrieked with pleasure, and came again, a huge spurt of semen filling my mouth.

He withdrew from me, gasping. Seth also withdrew, his form changing back to human. "Please, once more?" he said to Devlin, gasping. "As human?"

Screw what Devlin wanted! I wanted more! I was already stroking Seth's penis, which was again lengthening in my hand, as he let out a moan.

Devlin was stripping off his clothes. "Ride him," he said to me gutturally.

Seth rolled onto his back, and with an eager groan I slipped onto him. I was surprised he still felt so large, but he moved in me gently, suckling my breasts as he squeezed them in his hands. I pushed closer, feeling his organ within me completely. "Deeper," I groaned, moving on him. "I want your entire cock in me, every inch!"

Seth moaned, then pushed up with his hips, grasping my thighs to bury himself in me completely.

Then icy hands took hold of my hips. With a loud moan, I felt Devlin penetrate my ass, working the massive length of himself inside. I let out a scream, but Seth held me still, even as I struggled. "Stop!" I said desperately. "It's too big! You're too big!"

"You're as tight as your mother," Devlin moaned. "God, Danial was right to love this!"

I felt a wave of revulsion, and then they began to move, and I went limp on Seth, moaning as the feeling of being so filled to the brim engulfed me. *Oh God...both of them...it feels so good, I don't ever want it to stop, not ever...*

"See, you can take me, all of me!" Devlin whispered darkly. "And I'm going to come in you, Elle. I'm going to fuck you in your ass and you can't stop me! Because deep down, you want me to!"

"No!" I screamed silently. But I had no control over my mouth! "Yes!" I screamed out, my climax washing over me again. "Yes, I want you to! Please, please come in me! Please fuck me!"

Devlin hammered himself into me, growling, and Seth began growling too, also thrusting hard. A few moments later they came together.

Devlin withdrew from me carefully, and then we all went to the bathroom, and showered. I was full of semen by then, and it was seeping out of me steadily. I was scared to see Devlin had bloody smears on him, though if it was mine from him or his from my bites, I couldn't tell. But as the water washed us, my body healed, and soon we were clean. I told myself I was okay, that what had happened was new to me, but that people did this together, and it wasn't abnormal, it was just exotic.

When we finished, Seth gave me a gentle kiss. "I loved being with you," he said politely. "If you ever want to be together again, please call my cell." He paused. "I'll be cougar for you, if you need me to, like your brother does for Serena, if you'll be bear for me." Then he smiled. "And some of the other bears would love to join us, if you feel like taking on more than just me. I can get as many as you want for you to feel satisfied, Elle. Whatever you want, just tell me. I know your Mom likes three-on-one sometimes."

I nodded, even as my real self was screaming inside.

Seth left, and then I felt icy hands enclose me from behind, and force me to my knees.

"I planned this, niece," Devlin purred. "And since you let me and Seth fuck you so well, I'm glad I did."

His hands melted to paws, and then I heard a guttural roar. *A cougar's roar.* I turned to see Devlin had become a cougar. His organ was already extending and hardening as he watched me, purring.

I shifted fast, and the moment my body became cougar he was on me, penetrating me, his body riding mine to the ground as he pistoned in and out of me. *His organ is so huge and long! God, he feels so good! And his scent is prairie, and grass, and everything wild and free!*

I came within seconds, my roar shaking the room. His roar a few seconds later swallowed mine, it was so loud.

He fucked me for over an hour, his seed dripping out of me steadily, my body becoming raw. But I could not get enough of him. I'd never had one of my own kind before, never! *And it feels so good! It feels so right!*

Devlin finally eased off me, his breathing ragged. Exhausted, we curled around each other and went to sleep.

I thought when that happened I would wake up. But there was more to come.

I woke up in Devlin's arms, as human.

"Are you sore?" he asked pleasantly.

"No," I said, touching my clit and vagina carefully. "But I'm swimming in your seed. My scent isn't mine anymore, it's yours."

"I know," he said, taking a deep breath. "I can smell it inside you. I love the smell of my come in you." He kissed me. "I love the taste of my come in you."

I snuggled against him, and he kissed my forehead gently.

"Uncle, I—"

"No more 'uncle'," he said sharply. "We have crossed a line, Elle. You are a lover now, not a pretend family member. Call me Dev from now on."

"Dev, I want you. Will you not make love to me?"

"I've been violating you in all ways, my dear," he said in an evil voice. "And I intend to violate you still more, before we are done. But do you not want a rest?"

"No," I said throatily. "I want you. I want you to make love to me."

Devlin pulled me astride him, and then I finally felt his manhood enter me. He was larger than Seth, and he stretched me. And then he was stroking me in long movements, and I was swaying above him.

"Call out my name," he said, rocking my hips on his. "Call it out as you come!"

"Dev!" I gasped. "Oh Dev! Fuck me, Dev! Fuck me so deep and hard!"

Devlin laughed in a rich voice and then he rolled over on me, still thrusting.

"Bite me, Elle," he said in a voice heavy with lust. "Use your cougar fangs to bite me, as I come."

"I don't want to hurt you—"

"You won't, you'll give me the best orgasm with you so far. Do it!"

Devlin jerked in the next moment, and I bit down hard as I felt him come, and then he was shrieking out, over and over as he came. And when he rolled off of me, his penis finally softened.

"Shit, that was good," he groaned. He looked over at me. "God, it was just as good with you as I always knew it would be!"

"You were wonderful, too," I said, slurring my words a little. I was exhausted by now, and feeling weak from both the blood loss and phenomenal sex.

"Lay back," he said seriously. "One thing remains."

I lay back on the pillows for him. Without saying anything more, he bit down into my throat. He began swallowing my blood down greedily, his arms tightening around me as he nursed from me.

"Stop," I said weakly. "I feel like I'm dying!"

"You are," he whispered lovingly. "Don't fight it, Elle."

I struggled in his arms, but he resumed drinking. I began panicking as I grew weaker and weaker. "Stop, please! Please, don't hurt me!"

"I want to," he said lovingly, caressing my cheek. "I love werecougar blood, Elle. It's my favorite. I've never fucked a werecougar and not ended up draining her. I just can't resist!"

I tried to fight him, but he held me down, still swallowing. "Shh," he said gently. "Your heart is already faltering. A few more swallows and I'll end you."

"Why?" I gasped weakly. "Why are you doing this to me? How could you share what we did and do this to me?"

"Because I'm a sadist," Devlin said with a shrug. "And your mother would never forgive me for fucking you, even if Danial somehow did. So you'll be found in a few weeks at school, and a boy will be blamed, and punished for your murder. Leri will help me cover it up, she has before—"

"No, please! Please, Dev!"

"Goodbye, Elle," he said lovingly. "Please know it was nothing personal." He began drinking again, and I felt myself fading into nothingness…

I awoke screaming, my heart pounding, my body covered in sweat and the scent of my own come. I ran to the bathroom and vomited up everything in my stomach. After, I took a long hot shower, trying to pull myself together. When I emerged, I grabbed all of the bed linen, took them down to the laundry room, and got them washing. As I made the bed with fresh sheets, I tried to get my mind around that dream.

Devlin clearly had thought about being with me sexually, to have been able to dream up that elaborate of a fantasy. *Fucking me, and then killing me.* What had been in the dream had been what he'd wanted to happen, if he'd truly been free to do what he wanted, with no restraints. *Mother of Christ.*

I had to get out of here, as soon as possible. I could not live with him here, not even if it meant enduring Jenny's triteness and my father's dumbness. Anything was better than living with a sadist.

Chapter Four

I managed to avoid Devlin for most of the next day. But when it got to be nightfall, he found me in my room. "I wanted to apologize for the other night," he said hesitantly. "I want you to know I've been to see Serena, Elle, and I have…gotten out some of my frustrations."

He has no idea I was in the dream with him. "It's okay," I mumbled, unable to look at him.

"Please forgive me. I should have never let anything like that happen. I want to assure you that it will not ever happen again. You have my word, niece."

I nodded. "Thank you."

"Stay as long as you want, please." He closed the door behind him.

A moment later, Danial came in. I looked at my dad, smiling at me so earnestly, and immediately began bawling.

"What is it, daughter?" he said in a worried tone, rushing to my side and enfolding me in his arms. "Please don't cry. Tell me what's wrong. What happened?"

I cried harder, too horrified and embarrassed to confess any of the dream, or my own stupidity in choosing to dream with Devlin. My dad just held me, and told me it was okay, whatever it was would be okay, because he was there, and he would fix whatever it was that had me so upset, if I would just tell him what was wrong.

A half-hour later, I finally got myself under control, confident I had a good enough answer for him that would really be a fix to what had happened. "I'm okay now."

"What is it, daughter?"

"I…I want you to help me build a new home on Mom's property," I said quickly.

"Why?" he said in a curious tone. "Do you not like Hayden?"

"T said that Mom's yard is getting to be overgrown, and I know there was a lot of talk of selling it, though Mom didn't want to. But I would like to live there, Dad."

"When? After college?"

"I want to take a break from college," I said, cringing a little because I was sure he'd be disappointed or angry with me. "I want to garden, and maybe have a few horses. I know Mom had the barn, and it didn't burn, like the house."

My dad looked at me carefully. "Did something happen at school?"

"No. My classes just—"

"Did something happen here?" he interjected.

Did it ever. "No."

"Don't lie to me, daughter. What happened here?"

You knew it was hopeless to try to tell him a lie. But you can't tell him what really happened, either. "I need to be on my own for a while, maybe get some more therapy," I said quickly. "Please, Dad. Just a…a year, maybe less."

"Are you sure?" he said slowly. "What happened, Elle? You know you can tell me anything. I won't judge you."

Telling my father that I'd made a deal with a witch in order to have adventuresome sex with his deviant brother would appall and hurt my ultra-moral father. I also knew he would blame Devlin for this, though what had happened had in fact been my fault. Leri had warned me about Dev—not that I hadn't already known he was a sadist—and I hadn't listened. I'd just thought of my fantasy of Devlin, not of who he really was. Realizing that made me feel stupid, because I'd always known who he was, deep down. Once again, I'd chosen to see what I wanted to see in a man, and not what was really there.

"Elle, what happened?" my father persisted. "You must tell me."

At least there was another truth I could tell him as a reason for leaving. "I don't get along with V. She hates me, Dad, and the truth is I hate her, too. I have since the moment I laid eyes on her."

"Devlin and I hated one another sometimes when we were boys. It will pass."

"Maybe it will. But I need some time, especially with Mom being gone—"

"Your mother's death was a tragedy," Danial said, his eyes tearing up. "But she loved you, Elle. Do not doubt for one moment that she did—"

Here we go. Stop him before he gets started. "I don't. But I need some time to just think about things. The new house doesn't have to be a fancy home, just a trailer like mom had. If it's a problem with money, I can repay you—"

"Money is not an issue, daughter," Danial said with a snort. "Not when it comes to you. You know that well. But are you sure you want this? Sar was often lonely, after her husband died, before she met me. And in those months when we broke up, when she lived there alone. It's a remote place."

There were neighbors within a half-mile; I wanted to say, unlike Danial's home or Hayden, which had no neighbors for almost twenty. But I knew some of his cautioning was just him being protective of me. "I'm sure."

"Then I'll set something up. Devlin had already been considering building a home there for V, but you as the elder child have first rights. So I'll start things moving. When were you thinking of moving in?"

"In a week?"

Danial gave me a narrow-eyed look. "What happened, daughter? This is more than a fight with your half-sister. You are running scared of something. Tell me."

"I can't talk about it," I said flatly. "The short version is that I loved someone, and they betrayed me. And I need some time by myself to heal up my broken heart."

"Was it one of the bears?"

"No."

"Kyle?"

God, he was going to ask about Devlin next! "No, it was no one living here, Dad! Please drop it! I'll tell you about it when I can, I promise."

"I'll hold you to that," he said, nodding. "I'll go now, and begin arranging things. Please rest."

I sighed in relief as he closed the door. I stayed awake that night, afraid to sleep, lest I dream again.

* * * *

A week later, I moved into my new home. It was just a simple trailer, as my mother's house had been. But it was all mine, my first place, and it seemed almost like a palace to me.

Contractors had repaired the cracked foundation, and when that was done, a prefab doublewide had been lifted onto the existing foundation by a crane. And that was really all there was to it. Well, the pipes in the basement all had to be redone, but that was quickly finished, as was the rewiring of the electricity in the basement.

The next night, I moved in. My fathers both helped me, as did Jenny, Sun, and Terian. Most of the furniture was new, though I'd told Dad second hand was okay. But as usual he'd insisted, and I'd given in. At least it was just standard department store stuff, nothing expensive. I appreciated him doing this for me; I didn't want to act like a spoiled brat.

Devlin had been surprised to see the building moving along so fast. Though he told me he didn't understand why I was leaving Hayden, he also sent a piece of furniture as a farewell gift: a large flat screen TV.

Everyone but Danial ate some pizza after, and then they left, telling me not to become a hermit. When they left, I breathed a sigh of relief.

The next day, I was awakened by the sound of a tractor-trailer arriving. And driving it was Titus's demon brother, Rip. I gave him a hug before he got out from behind the wheel. "What are you doing here?"

"Devlin asked me to bring this for you," he said shrugging. "He said you might need it here."

I looked inside the trailer, and there was my mother's lawn tractor and her large farm tractor, too, as well as the log splitter, and her chainsaws. Associated gas cans, tools, chains, oil, and other bits of farm equipment were in some plastic tubs, too.

I felt instantly worried, to be taking possession of my mother's stuff, as if she really were gone for good. *Does Devlin know my mom isn't coming back?* "Why now?"

"He said they would do you more good here than in storage at Hayden," Rip said in a soft tone. "He was very emotional about it."

They would be useful. Don't think about any other ramifications. "Okay, help me put them in the barn."

Rip lifted most of the heavy things, and I drove the tractors down, towing the log splitter. My mother had showed me what to do that long ago summer we'd stayed here with Dad, though I'd fought her tooth and nail all the way. I'd been so sure back then that I was never going to want to live here in the sticks, not when I could live with my father in grand style. I'd been real sure about a lot of things.

I wiped away a few tears of my own, as I got down off the tractor.

"I wasn't sure if you knew," Rip said uneasily, trying not to look at me crying. "But there is wood here." He said a few words, and the woodshed that had appeared empty suddenly was entirely filled with wood. Some of it looked a little rotted, but most looked okay. "Titus hid it, since no one was living here. Lash, Sar, and some guards cut it, a while ago."

That was a big relief. I bit my lip, wishing I could thank my mom and Lash, and wondering if there would ever come a time when I could. "Thanks."

"Your father said to tell you to make sure to leave your phone on. He wants to hear from you every night 'without exception.' And he also said to tell you that cable people have switched on your service, and that the furnace will be installed in a week. The woodstove will be coming in a month or so."

"Am I doing the right thing?" I asked him suddenly. "I don't have a job, Rip. I'm getting all this done for me because I'm Danial's daughter. If it was up to Theo, I'm sure I wouldn't be getting any of this, even if he could afford it. Is this fair, to take advantage of my adoptive father's wealth?"

"I'm not sure," Rip said after a moment. "I make no pretense of being as good as my brother Titus. My motto's been 'take what you can, when you can.' But it's not like Danial's hurting for money, Elle. And if you think V is going to ever not get everything she wants, that's bullshit. So why shouldn't you get this house, and a little time to decide what you want out of life? And who said you couldn't take online classes while you're here, or maybe get a dog, or get some kind of part-time job?"

What wonderful ideas! I looked at him in amazement, and then hugged him.

"What'd I say?" he said uncomfortably.

"Never mind," I mumbled, crying again. "Never mind. Just hug me."

* * * *

The next week, I took his advice, and tried some projects. I dug up the flower gardens that were full of weeds now, and cleared room for the irises and other perennials to blossom. I went to the local library every week, and got a few books, which I read lying on the lawn in the sun, or inside on my couch on rainy days. I'd always liked astronomy, and so I took a class at the local community college, and then signed up for a few more math courses online. Between all that and taking care of my new house, including mowing the lawn, I kept busy.

I thought of getting a pet, but decided it was too much responsibility. I wasn't sure if I wanted anything depending on me. I liked the freedom of coming and going at all hours, even if it was just for walks in the local parks, or movies alone late at night. I knew a pet wasn't something I could take back if it didn't work out, and not hear flak from my mother for the rest of my life over it.

My mother and Lash were still missing. But I prayed for her, and kept believing that Lash would find a way to bring her home. And the summer slowly passed.

Everything was good until Elijah showed up one day out of the blue. I was mowing along, and thinking about what to watch tonight on TV, and there he was, standing in front of me on my lawn with his demon at his shoulder, frowning.

I swerved with a growl, and turned off the tractor.

He came toward me hesitantly. "Elle?"

"What are you doing here?" I demanded.

"I came to see you," he said in an obvious voice. "I missed you."

"V not giving you any?"

Elijah looked confused. "Why would she be giving me anything? We aren't friends."

"You looked pretty cozy that day I saw her going down on you."

Elijah looked at me with disgust, and a little sadness. "Why are you talking like that, in such a crude way? Ladies don't talk like that."

"Who said I was a lady?" I said hotly. "I'm sure your father didn't."

"He didn't," Elijah said flatly. "But I told him he was wrong, because I wanted him to be wrong. I wanted you to be sweet, like you were to me last spring when I visited you."

"I'm were," I said growling. "I'm not sweet. Any sweetness was torn out of me a year ago. There's only hardness left."

I thought Elijah would leave, but instead he came to me, and hugged me. "I'm sorry that happened to you, Elle. I'm sorry you remember it. But please don't think it makes you less in any way. You are still beautiful. You are still good."

I felt some of my distantness melting in the warmness of his goodwill, even as I felt relief that he knew what had happened to me, I wouldn't ever have to worry about telling him, and his reaction to my assault. "I tried to contact you."

"I know," Elijah said. "I was able to access your messages just recently."

"What took you so long? I left them months ago!"

"My mother had my phone," he said in a cold voice. "She was trying to call my father for help when hunters staked her. I saw her die, Elle. It wasn't pretty. The phone was destroyed in the process, because it was soaked in her blood."

"I'm sorry," I apologized, stunned. "I lost my birth mom, too. I never got to know her."

"You had Sar, at least," Elijah said bitterly. "I have only a father whose every waking moment is consumed by the need to control everything he touches."

Now was probably not the time to tell Elijah that I agreed with him about his father. "Come in. Do you want some lunch?"

"Sure," he said awkwardly. "But just a little. I've been losing my tolerance for human food."

I concentrated hard on not giving him a pitying look, and walked inside. I made us some lunch of ham sandwiches and mustard. We ate, but Elijah finished only half of his. I took the plates away, stuck them in the sink, and we went out onto the lawn, the demon following. Dusk was falling, and the bats were out circling the house, eating insects.

"So what have you been doing?" I asked. "Plans for college?"

"I don't know what I want," Elijah whispered. "Everything seems to be so tenuous that's good. And the things that last are all bad."

"What do you mean?"

"I want the world to stop spinning, to slow down. I'm tired of being hunted by obsessive humans, with having a demon haunt my every footstep! I want to be normal, to have someone to care about me, and not to look at me like either something to be feared or a freak."

"You aren't a freak."

"I am," he said, redness shining in his eyes. "I'm just a tool for vampires to use. That's all I am to my father. And that's all I'll ever be."

"Not to me." I kissed him, and he responded slowly. Then he was rolling over on me, pressing against me, as his mouth devoured mine. When he slid his hands under my shirt, I didn't stop him. His hands caressed me gently through my bra, but I felt all the power of his desire in the way he trembled slightly, as he squeezed my breasts in his hands. When he slid his hands under my bra and tweaked my nipples, I let out a primal moan of longing. Then I was fumbling with his shirt, and he was breathing hard, helping me push it back, and I ran my fingers over his hard chest. It was sculpted, the muscles like large warm rocks rolling easily under my hands.

God, I have to get his clothes off! I tugged at his belt, and pulled open his zipper, and saw the hard length of him pushing against his boxers. I put my hand on him, and he reacted as though I'd shocked him, jerking up under me with a cry.

But when I tried to pull down his underwear, he stopped me. "No. We can't."

I gave him a look that told him he had to be kidding me. "We're adults. We can."

"We aren't Oathed," he said, shaking his head. "Or married. I don't want to have sex until I am one of those, Elle."

I lost it, just like that. "You let V deep throat you okay, when she looked only five! Where was all that self-restraint then?"

Elijah gave me a look of disgust, and got up, putting his clothes on. "I told you I never did that. I've never touched her, not ever! I liked you. I was ever only intimate with you, tonight!"

"I saw you! Don't lie to me, Elijah!"

"I'll go," he said in a cool tone. "If you won't believe I'm telling you truth, there's no point in me speaking to you."

"Get out," I said flatly, straightening my clothes. "Get out, damn you."

Elijah gave me a last look and left. Harp emerged from the shadows, and took his hand, and they disappeared.

* * * *

I thought about what had happened in every free moment for the next week.

Maybe I shouldn't have brought up what I saw. But damn it, he could have just admitted it to me! He could have said it was just sex, and I'd have said fine, it's not like we'd ever said we wouldn't see other people! He didn't have to pretend it hadn't happened, not when I'd seen it with my own eyes!

I decided to go out for a run in the forest that night. That was fine, until I was bounding along, finally feeling kind of happy and came down with my left paw squarely in a bear trap.

The pain was agonizing, and I roared loudly once before I stifled myself. Telling myself to remain silent, in case someone had heard me, I changed form, and looked at my hurt hand. With difficulty, I pried open the trap's lever, and got my hand out. But my hand was mangled now. My bones had healed the fracture, but there was a limit to how much healing could be done in one night, and deep gashes ran the length of my palm, and across the back of my hand.

I scented a human nearby on the autumn wind, just as it began to pour. Afraid, I changed form again to cougar, and limped back towards my house, grateful for the rain to cover my tracks. I got inside as fast as possible, and hurried to the bathroom, scared to look at my hand, but knowing I had to. Close inspection revealed that my hand was healed, but I couldn't use my fingers well. *God, have the nerves been severed? What should I do?*

My father Theo had been tortured once, and recovered. I'd heard it had been extremely bad, and had taken months to heal. But I didn't want to call him, even if he would come give me his opinion. Who I wanted to call was Lash, but he was still missing with my mother. So I'd have to call Dad, which would mean not only a lecture, but probably him arranging to kill the person who'd done this to me, and then moving back to his estate to live with Theo and Jenny, or living at Hayden with Dev and V...*no.*

I bit my lip. *Screw it, who says I have to call anyone for help?* My mother had been here alone, and not had anyone to call when Danial had bitten her. She had bandaged herself up and gone to bed. So who the hell said I needed to call anybody either? *I can handle this.*

I put a bandage on my hand, made sure my doors were all locked, and went to bed.

* * * *

The next day, I went out and posted my land with no trespassing signs. Well, technically it was still my mom's land, but I was thinking of it as mine now. I found another trap, when I put my animal nose to use and looked for the scent that didn't belong. Animals weren't smart enough to think if something had no scent at all it might be dangerous, or if it smelled like concentrated old cougar pee. But I was. So I disabled the trap, and then followed the trail back to the human's home who'd put them there on my land. "These yours?" I said, tossing them down on his tiny porch in front of him.

"Yes," he said, stubbing out his cigarette. "I've had two lambs killed in the last month, not even found their bodies. There's a bear around here, some say. But I swore I heard a cougar last night."

"It's probably the coyotes," I said, thinking fast. "I've heard them at night."

"Something bigger," he said, shaking his head. "I've seen tracks. They're on your land, but also all around here. We've got some big predator here for sure, Missy."

Shit. He must have a bear on his land for real. "Look, I feel bad you lost livestock. But I walk in the woods, and I don't want to hurt my foot. As it was, your trap going off scared me so much I fell and landed on my hand and sprained it."

He looked contrite. "Sorry, Ma'am. But until this bear's caught, you might do well to stay out of the woods."

Right. I was going to have to go out nightly now, until I found whoever or whatever was killing the lambs, before they blew my cover.

Chapter Five

I went out that night on patrol, and saw absolutely nothing. So I went back to my normal day walks, and changed in the barn as a cougar for a week, playing it safe. I found no more traps in my woods, when I looked the next week. So I considered the matter settled, and turned my thoughts back to college. I registered for a few more math courses, and threw in some on botany and cell structure for variety.

Then one night in early September, I got a call from my father Theo that told me my mother was back, that she'd been found. I made sure I was there to welcome her home. It was so good to be back in her arms. Sure V was there, too, but I ignored her.

But when I went to see Sar in the following weeks, she was always busy doing something. Though I left messages, she never returned them. Even my dad was distant, not calling to check on me as he always had before her return. I buried myself in new classes, but it didn't help my sadness.

A month passed, September becoming early October. I felt lonely, lonely enough to go to Danial's home to see if the foxes were there. They were, but running with them didn't slake my urge to mate, which was overpowering now. As always, there was no one there like me.

Part of me was tempted to call Seth, to ask him if he would be cougar for me. Devlin had chosen him to be with me for some reason in the dream, likely for his gentleness, so maybe it would be okay to be with him in real life. If reality was anything like the dream of him, he could fill my void with aplomb. But I was too embarrassed to just call him up and ask out of the blue to hook up, so I never contacted him.

Things got better a little while after that, when Devlin finally heard his darling daughter mouthing off to me one afternoon. My mother also heard it, and punished V. But even after that happened, mom still seemed busy, usually spending time with Devlin's resurrected witch love, Rene. Though Rene acted very kindly toward me in the moments I saw her, her presence all the time made me stay away from my mother.

Finally, in mid-October, I began to act erratically, the pressure from being alone so much finally wearing me thin as tissue paper. I'd pace in the barn as cougar, until my legs were sore, and I was panting. Finally, to stop my relentless mad pacing, I began going into the woods as cougar most nights. There I lay in the woods and felt peaceful, falling asleep under a huge oak tree most nights.

That made my existence bearable, until a morning in early November when I woke up in a cage.

Oh shit! I looked around, and saw a place I didn't know. It was a small room, with what looked like metal walls. There was the stink of animals, other big cats and bears and something else, but no animals were in evidence. A large overhead door was open some yards away, daylight shining outside. *Where am I? A warehouse?*

Voices were outside, just barely audible. "Look what we found last night! A cougar! Can you believe it?"

"It'll bring us a few grand easy. Lots of people will pay for a hide, and even for the meat—"

Shit!

"No, it'd be better to sell her to a game farm! Dose her up, and she'll be a sitting duck! And her body's great, she'd make a sweet trophy—"

I lay down in the cage and wanted to cry, listening to them fight over me. Part of me wanted to change, rationalizing that maybe if they saw I was a woman, they'd let me out. *That is wishful thinking. They'll just sell me for more to a lab for study.*

I lay there for a day and a night with no food or water, feeling

67

shame as I'd had to go to the bathroom, and my offal was left there with me in the cage to reek. I cried on and off, trying to make a plan of attack, wondering if I could bear the pain of getting shot in order to break free.

That night, I heard a truck backing up towards me to the open overhead door, its lights red glowing eyes in the gloom. A man rinsed out my cage with a hose, getting me soaked in the process. I hissed at him, but he ignored me, heading back outside.

"She's all yours, bud," the man said to someone. "Thanks for the cash."

They loaded me in the truck with a forklift as I snarled, and then I was being driven away into the night. We drove for at least three hours. Then the truck stopped, and I heard footsteps.

Where am I? God, I am going to have to kill someone to break free. But I can do it, right? Mom did it to defend me, and her. I just have to not think about it.

The door rolled up, I gathered myself to strike the moment they came close, and then I was blinking in bright light hearing a familiar voice.

"Didn't I fucking tell you not to change in the fucking forest?"

Lash stood there, looking pissed. He'd driven me back to my own land. I let out a joyful roar, and began purring.

"Sure, you purr now! How about I spank your ass? Your mom's been worried, and so is Danial." He released my cage door, and I hopped out, and began to shake some of the water off me.

"Don't you fucking dare!" he yelled, getting out of range. "Get inside and shower. You smell like shit! Right now, Elle!"

I slunk inside and showered, feeling so good to be clean. When I came out, I saw Lash'd brought us both a half a pig, and he was eating some raw bacon. "There's a plate for you," he said. "Eat, you must be starving."

Famished, I got a plate, and gorged myself. Before long, we'd finished most of the pig.

"Thanks," I said, and before I could get out any more words, I broke down crying again. With an irritated hiss, Lash hugged me. I scented his sickening snake aroma, but I pushed down my feelings of revulsion, and hugged him hard.

"You're a pain in my ass, just like your mother," he grumbled. Then he kissed me on my forehead.

"Thanks for saving me."

"I didn't save you, I bought you," Lash hissed. "Five G's, Elle. That's what your life was worth. I had to outbid a breeder on the black market version of E-bay, not to mention a man who wanted you just for a stuffed trophy."

"I'll pay you back," I vowed staunchly.

"With what?" he said, rolling his eyes. "You don't have a job. And I don't want that fuck Danial's money—"

"With myself," I said boldly, and then I kissed him. "Anything you want, it's yours."

Lash was so shocked he dropped his empty whiskey glass, and it took him almost a minute to grab hold of it and push me away. "Stop, Elle. Right now."

"Please," I whispered. "I'm so lonely, Lash. There's nobody here like me. You must have felt like this before yourself. Nobody wants me. Nobody. I feel like I'm dying of loneliness."

Lash looked down at me for a moment, and then he gave me a deep kiss, winding his human tongue around mine. I lost myself in it, and it went on and on, and he held me in his strong arms. Before long I could feel he was as excited as I was, but when I reached down for him, to stroke him, he stopped me.

"No," he said, moving back from me. "If I wasn't mated, we'd already be on our second time, Elle. Any male would want you, werecougar or not. You're just lonely. Now, what happened with Elijah?"

"How do you know all this? In fact, how'd you find me?"

"I make it my business to know," Lash hissed darkly. "I know of what goes on, and who deals in black market stuff. And what I don't know, Dev does, especially when it has to do with weres."

"Did you stop them? They had other animals there, Lash, before me. I smelled another lion and some kind of jaguar—"

"They deal deer meat, and some bear and coyote skins. And some exotic animals that've been imported from other states headed to game farms out west. No, I didn't. This goes on, Elle, and I'm not a hero. I was there to save you and you only."

"How could you leave them there to be shot? I thought you were a good guy."

"Whatever gave you that idea?" Lash said with a grin. Then he saw how upset I was, and let out a sigh. "Look, Elle, I know those guys. Because I do business with them, they let me know as a courtesy when they find something odd around this area. And that's how it stays. Killing them is the only way to stop them, and then someone new would just come in and start up the business. And the next time this happened, I might not hear about it until whatever were it was got killed, or found out to be more than an animal. Sometimes some animals have to die. That's the price for the were community staying free, the price of you and I staying free. Because nothing is ever really free in life, it all comes with a price tag; it just depends on whether you can pay that price. And the sad truth is that some can, and some can't. You understand that?"

"No," I said, hurt. "I don't. People have to do what's right, no matter the cost. And you should have saved those animals from being killed. I don't understand!"

"Your mother does," Lash said in an ancient voice. "She understands why I did what I did, even if she doesn't like it. And if you think a little on what I said tonight, you will, too. Now get off me, my dick's uncomfortably hard and twisted up."

I blushed, and got up, and he got to his feet with a groan, arranging himself.

"Call Elijah," he said, putting on his coat. "He liked you a lot. He'd probably be werecat for you if you asked him to."

"I can't. He lied to me, saying he'd never been with V—"

"He hasn't been. V's a virgin," Lash said easily. "Devlin's been keeping tabs on that closely, trust me."

"It happened at Samuel's. And it wasn't regular sex—"

"Nothing happened," Lash hissed angrily. "V is watched at all times by someone, no matter where she is."

"The demon wasn't watching. He was downstairs with the kitchen maid getting some."

Lash laughed. "Then he was watching from afar, as Titus often does. Nothing happened—"

"I fucking saw her going down on him, Lash. Don't fucking tell me it didn't happen!"

Lash gave me a considering look. "Think about this, Elle: Samuel hates weres, werecougars in particular, because of your father Theo's former relationship with Sar. He knows his son had feelings for you. And he has a demon who does magic under his employ. Anything adding up for you here?"

I couldn't speak. "You're saying this was a trick? That Samuel tricked me?"

"Likely. But you'd have to ask Elijah, and believe he'll tell you the truth."

I couldn't face Elijah, not after what'd happened, how I'd acted. "Stay here with me," I said, hugging him quickly. "Please. I don't want to be alone."

"No," Lash hissed gently, disentangling himself. "One thing might lead to another. I'm not the poster child for restraint or good judgment, not when I'm horny. And your mom's waiting for me."

"Then why'd you kiss me?" I said angrily. "You kissed me, Lash!"

"I like to kiss," Lash hissed with a grin. "And you needed one, a good one done right." He touched my cheek gently. "I remember being lonely, remember being close to dying and thinking there was not one female who gave a shit about me, much less wanted to be there to comfort me. I remember a lot of times through the years wanting to be comforted and having no one who'd touch me. And I wanted you to know that you are never going to be like that, Elle. You're too damn hot." He laughed. "Believe me; I'd do more than kiss you if I wasn't mated. So you shouldn't feel like no one wants—"

"What I feel is that you were hard for me," I said, my hand darting out and grabbing his crotch, as he let out an "Oof" of surprise. "You're still hard."

"I get hard just watching the Discovery Channel, if it's on venomous snakes," Lash said with a chuckle, moving my hand off him. "And like I told you, you're hot. But even if you aren't my daughter, you're my mate's daughter." His eyes flattened briefly. "So no more grabbing me, ever, got it?"

I nodded, ashamed. "I'm sorry. You're right, I shouldn't have."

"I'm sorry for making things confused for you. I'm not the best at knowing what to say and do." He hugged me briefly, and let me go. "Call Elijah, he'll come here and give you what you need. But first load your gun and lock your door. An empty gun's like a man with a limp dick: useless."

He strode out into the night. A moment later his truck started up. Then his headlights were gone, roaring out my long driveway.

I let out a sigh. And I made sure my .20-gauge shotgun was loaded, and the door was locked before I turned in for bed.

I was awakened only a few hours later by the ringing phone.

"Hello?"

"Elle, its Sharon. Remember me?"

I blinked my eyes. Sharon, sure, a girl from England. She'd been in one of my online classes. We'd chatted online, and studied together. I'd given her my number and told her to come enjoy the country life, but she'd never visited. But the way she talked about her life, her parents were very domineering, at least her father was. "Hi."

"You said I could stay with you. Would you mind if I did?"

"Sure. When will you be in town?"

"I'm outside your door now."

I sat bolt upright in bed, feeling too scared to breathe. "You're here now? How? I didn't hear a car drive up—"

"Please, Elle. I'm exhausted."

I got my gun, and went to the door. There I found Sharon, who looked sweet and a little cowed. With her was a man whose reeking blackness told me he was demon before I ever opened the door.

"This is Song," Sharon said hurriedly. "He won't hurt you, Elle. May we come in?"

"Why the hell do you have a demon? Who are you?" I said, cocking the gun, and putting my finger on the trigger.

Sharon looked at me a little sadly, and then she opened her mouth, to reveal fangs. "I'm Elijah's sister."

"I thought you hated werecreatures," I said in a growling voice, not moving a muscle. "I thought I was beneath you. So why should I open my door and give you a place to sleep?"

"I don't think you're less than me," Sharon said, cowed. "I thought we'd become friends over the last few months. You invited me to stay sometime. So, I came to you, because next to V, you're the only friend I have. And going to Devlin's house might cause some kind of inter-Ruler incident."

"The demon stays outside. But come in if you want to."

Sharon nodded to Song, who shrugged, and disappeared. Elijah's sister came inside, and I gave her a blanket, because it was snowing by now, and she was wet.

"Can I stay for a few days?" she said.

"Sure," I said. "I have a spare bedroom. But you have to tell me why you're here. I don't want your father coming here, and breaking my door down looking for you."

"He doesn't know we know each other. And Song is bound to me, not him. So he'll guard us, and warn us if anyone comes near."

"Is his real name 'Song'?"

"Bloodsong. I don't know why. But I don't know why my brother's demon was called Harp either. Neither of them seem to like music—"

I didn't care about that. "Why are you here?"

"Elijah has been fighting with my father on and off for months. But they had a huge fight the night of All Hallows Eve, and Elijah left the estate that night and hasn't returned."

I was immediately worried about him, even as I told myself not to be. "Where is he?"

"I don't know. I'm hoping he's been staying with your brother, T. They were talking a lot the night of the party." She snorted. "My father would love that."

"Why do you say that?"

"Because my father just adores your brother. He wanted a son who'd be just like T is to Danial: the doting son, following in the family business, a younger version of himself with the best of human and vampire." She smiled bitterly. "Instead he got us, the vampire kids who have red eyes and fangs, and age abnormally fast."

Shit, how to ask what I need to ask? "Are you still able to eat food? I have some if you're hungry."

"A little," Sharon said sadly. "I miss it. But I need blood now. And I can eat liquefied meat, too."

"Then we should be able to get along okay," I laughed. "I like raw meat, too."

Sharon smiled. "I can pay some of the expenses. I have some money in a bank."

"Won't your father be angry?"

Sharon shook her head. "I think he'll be relieved. He wants me out from underfoot, so he can concentrate on finding Elijah."

I got out a beef roast, and handed her half of it. She cut hers into chunks and processed them in the blender, and then came over to sit with me at the table. We ate without speaking, as she was clearly very hungry, and I was still trying to think of something to say that didn't mention Elijah.

When we'd finished, she washed our dishes, dried them, and put them away. And then I poured her some wine, and some for myself, and we sat near the fire, talking.

I was warm, full, and pretty happy, having escaped death and gained some company in the same night. So, I didn't pay attention to how much I'd drank, especially as I'd eaten a huge meal earlier, plus a smaller one less than an hour ago. Sharon only had a little liquid, and the alcohol hit her like a ton of bricks. Within an hour, she was telling me her life story, about how her mother had been a delicate, shallow, and emotionally distant figure she had only a few memories of.

"Sure some of that was she'd been broken by my father," she concluded bitterly. "I heard about it from things I overheard, even if neither of my parents ever talked about it. But some of that was just her loving the status that being my mother gave her." She downed her wine, and poured herself the rest of the bottle. "She was less interested in being a mother and more interested in being a queen."

I nodded, thinking about my mother. Sure, she hadn't been mother of the year, but I'd always known she cared about me. *But my biological father, well...* "Theo always is nice to me," I said after a moment. "For a long time, I told myself that he was distant because of the spells he'd had put on him, that they'd caused him to put me second." I finished my wine. "But the truth is, he's got no spell on him now, and he's the same as he used to be; the loving father when I'm around and right out of his mind the second I'm not." I smiled. "But my Dad, Danial, he's always been there for me. He's the one who bought me this house."

"My father could never understand that," Sharon slurred. "He thought once Danial had T, he'd forget about you."

I laughed. "That's never happened."

Sharon gave me a sad smile. "I know. I'm so jealous of you." She held my gaze for a moment, and then burst into tears.

Shit. I went to her and hugged her awkwardly. "Shh, it's okay. Stop crying—"

"I hoped after my mother died that my father would get Sarelle to come be with him," Sharon sobbed. "I knew she'd had vampire children before, so she'd understand us better." She cast me a guilty look. "I heard him talking to Perseus, Elle. He knows your mother's able to have children again."

I felt momentary fear, and then it dissipated. "Everyone's going to know soon anyway, Sharon. Lash and my mother are trying for a baby."

Sharon choked on her wine, spattering it all over the floor, and on the throw pillow. I gave her an irritated look, and went in search of a towel. When I got back, she'd finished her wine, and I wiped up the mess, glad I'd had vinyl floors put in here and not carpet.

"My father'll go insane," Sharon said finally. "He forbade her having any non-vampire children; at least, that's what Song told me."

"Lash and Devlin will handle it," I said confidently. "They wouldn't have done this unless they could."

"I feel sick," Sharon said, getting up slowly. "I should go to bed."

"Do you need to be in a room without sunlight?" I offered. "The guest bedroom has a window. But I can inflate a bed downstairs—"

"Not yet," Sharon murmured. "I'll be fine in a normal room."

I helped her to bed, and then turned in myself. It had been a hell of a long day.

* * * *

The next day Sharon was as friendly as she'd been online, and we quickly took up right where our online friendship had left off. She was also a big help, especially when the first real snowstorm hit the first week of December, dropping a foot of snow on us.

As for the demon, Song, I saw him little. He did come inside on the nights it dropped below 0 degrees, and I was grateful for his warmth. But I made him stay in Sharon's room with her when we went to bed. And when his brother Harp showed up to visit him, I made him stay with Sharon in her room, too.

I wondered that they didn't have some sort of relationship, being that she was able to sleep with him in the same room alone. But she never alluded to anything.

It was two weeks to the day she'd arrived when Elijah stopped by with his demon, Harp.

There had been a knock at the door, and I'd gone to get it, figuring it was a neighbor checking in with me. Some of my friendlier ones kept tabs on me, which I thought was sweet. I knew it was because they thought of me as vulnerable, because I lived alone. *Another snowstorm is forecast for this very evening.* But instead it was Elijah on my stoop, looking just as fabulous as he'd looked months ago. "Hi," he said a little abruptly. "Is my sister here?"

I nodded, and when he asked if he could come in, I nodded again.

Sharon gave him a big hug when she saw him. And I said quickly that I was going for a walk, and would be back in an hour.

I walked through the drifts of snow, glad of my powerful

werecougar body that made the heavy snow seem more of an inconvenience instead of a major hassle. I was far more hassled by my thoughts of Elijah. It was my daydreaming of him that got me hurt, when a dog attacked me out of nowhere.

I was blindsided, it happened so fast. But the sharp pain as its teeth grated on my forearm made me react without thinking. I whipped with all my strength to the side, throwing the dog against a nearby tree, breaking its back with a yelp. But my eyes weren't on it; they were on the other five ragged looking dogs surrounding me.

Shit. By appearance, these were all starving dogs that had been dumped out here by their owners, left to fend for themselves. In summer, they'd found each other, and survived with all the leavings of campers, because food was plentiful. But winter was here now, and so were the coyotes. Against the coyotes, the dogs had taken their only chance at survival, and formed a pack of their own. *A pack that is starving.*

A gun would've frightened them off with no problem. But mine was back at the house. *Shit.*

Two attacked from the front just as I melted to cougar.

I struck one a blow with a clawed hand that laid it open, the entrails splashing in a pile to lay beside its twitching form. But the other, a hound-shepherd, sunk its teeth into my right shoulder just as I felt more teeth close on my legs. I kicked out and heard a squeal of pain, and bit down on the dog on my shoulder, crushing its spinal cord. I dropped that one, and turned, grabbing the one latched onto my foot in my jaws and crushing him. The last one turned and ran. It got twenty feet before I came down hard on its back, breaking its spine.

I sat on my haunches, licking my lips. Blood was blood to me, and it tasted good, being so fresh. So, I ate some of the carcasses, and then dragged the bodies into my woods, where the coyotes would find them before long and clean them up. Sure, I could bury them in the snow, but there was no point. As I was dragging the last one, I noticed it was female. From the smell of it, it was also lactating.

I felt bad immediately, even knowing I'd only been defending myself. I carefully tracked the dog scent back over two miles and finally found the den in a thicket of scrub and thorn trees. The pups inside were dead, thin little skeletons covered in fur. Saddened, I went to leave when I heard a tiny "huff."

I nosed in the back of the den in a pile of thick hair, and found one last puppy, a female. She was terrified of me, growling, and baring her teeth even though she wobbled from hunger just trying to keep standing. I grabbed her by the scruff of the neck, and she curled her tail up around her body, though she kept growling. Carrying the puppy, I retraced my steps quickly, glad for the fresh snow that began to fall to cover my tracks.

When I got back to the scene of the fight, I gathered up the scraps of my clothes and my shoes, and transferred the still growling puppy to my human arms. Wet and shivering, I ran as fast as I could back to the house.

Sharon was there, but Elijah had left. For a fleeting moment, I was relieved but sad, and then reminded myself I had other things to think about. "Can you take her? I need to get some clothes on, and get the blood off me."

Sharon took the puppy, which stopped growling as soon as she gave it some meat. By the time I'd come out from showering, the puppy was snoozing on her lap, its belly bulging. I had some meat, and related the story to her of what had happened with the feral dogs. When I'd finished, I asked her how she felt about dogs as pets.

"Can we call her 'Hope'?" Sharon said as she petted the puppy.

"Sure," I said with a large grin. "We can always use more hope in our lives."

Chapter Six

The next week passed quickly. At its end, out of the blue, I had another surprise visitor: Danial.

He drove up in his Expedition pulling a double horse trailer. Before I even got out there to say hello, he was giving directions for some men to begin loading hay from two trucks that had tailed him here into the barn.

"Dad, what is all this?" I asked.

Danial turned to me, and I could tell immediately that he was angry, though his voice was its usual composed self. "I've brought you Poe and Annabelle Lee. I've also arranged for enough food for them. I picked up water buckets too—"

"Why bring them here? Devlin has stalls—"

"I'm moving back into my own house," he rasped, unlocking his back doors, and grabbing buckets and tack. "I don't want the horses at Hayden."

I grabbed some of the equipment to help him, and followed him into the barn. "Why now? You talked about going to Rule another state."

"I have realized Sar is Lady," he said brutally "Much to my chagrin and sorrow." He hung up the tack, and went back for more.

And the reunion didn't go well, sigh. Big surprise. I decided to just help and not talk. Together, we unloaded the rest of the tack, and hung it up. By that time, the men had lifted all the hay into the loft, and Danial paid them off. Their truck left ruts in the snow as it drove off, followed by the larger hay truck.

We prepared two stalls, getting the bedding down and the buckets in place. And then Danial led in the two horses in their blankets, and got them comfortable in adjoining stalls. "You are in good hands," he said to Poe comfortingly. "Rest easy."

"Do you want to come inside?" I said hesitantly. "We could talk."

Danial nodded.

I shut off the light, and we walked back to the house.

"Do you want to tell me what happened?" I said.

"No," Danial said in an old tone. "I don't." He pulled me into his arms and gave me a big hug. "Tell me instead of how you are. You look well. Country living agrees with you."

"I'm okay," I said with surety. "I got a dog. Her name's Hope."

Sure enough, Hope was already there at the door, whining. Danial picked her up at once and hugged her. Then he sat in the chair by the fire. "She's cute. Where did you get her?"

I related to him the story of the dog attack, and finding the puppy.

"You are just like your mother," Danial said in admiration. "Always saving the helpless." A sudden shadow passed over his face. "And how are your classes?"

I told of my A's and B's in my online courses, and he nodded in approval. "Who is living here with you?"

"Sharon," I said. *Shit, I should have known he'd scent demon.* "She's become a good friend."

"And her brother?"

"He visited once."

My father was still watching me closely. "And?"

"And nothing. He talked to Sharon in private, and then he left."

"As I should," Danial said, getting to his feet. "I have a long drive ahead of me back to my house. I'm not sure how things will go when I get there."

"What are your plans?"

"To save my company from foundering and get your brother back on track. And to call in a few favors to deal with some problems that have gone on far too long."

My father's tone was angry again. All at once, I knew what had him so furious: he'd fought with mom over Lash. "Favors for what?"

"For expediting what needs to be done," he said simply. "So please call the house if you need me from now on, Elle. My cell phone number is the same as it has been. And I'll be around weekly to ride Poe, if you're interested in accompanying me."

He gave me a hug, and left. As I watched him drive off, I thought to myself bitterly that he'd chosen to lock away his feelings for Sar inside his heart, as he always did when confronted with a person who didn't live up to his high expectations.

* * * *

The next week was quiet. Part of me wanted to call Mom and Lash and let them know Danial was planning something. But I knew Lash was smart enough to think of that himself, and so I never made the call.

Sharon and I cut down a spruce tree in my woods, and decorated it. Hope helped by barking encouragement to us. We sipped wine that night in front of the fire watching the tree lights blink on and off, and were content.

A few days later, my dad arrived. Danial and I spent a relaxing evening riding the horses over the fields at a slow pace. We talked a little, but not much, and he didn't mention Sarelle or Lash once.

Two days before Christmas, I returned from shopping to find a note from Sharon.

Freedom: Elle's Story

Elle,

I have been summoned home by my father for the holidays. I must go. Please hug Hope for me. I'll be back the day after New Years.

Sharon (and Song)

Bitch. I crumpled her note and threw it in the fire, angry at having been abandoned. Then I admitted that this was better, as I'd kind of had my own plans anyway for the holidays. I knew that I'd need to see my father and T, and also my mom, Lash, and Devlin, not to mention Theo and Jenny. *But I've gotten used to having Sharon to talk to, and I'm already missing her…*

There was a knock at the door. I peered out to see Elijah standing there, sans demon. I opened the door. "Your sister's not here."

"I'm here to see you," he said, his eyes fastened on me. "Can I come in?"

I nodded, and let him in. When we were sitting in front of the fire, he spoke. "I'm sorry about how we fought," he said earnestly. "I found out from Harp a while ago that he staged that scene you saw."

"I suspected that," I murmured.

"I've broken with my father," Elijah said sadly. "We've fought all fall, and last time he said some things I can't forgive. So Harp's with him now. I broke his bond to me."

"Should I be worried that he'll come after me?" I joked. "I know your father doesn't like me."

"That's why I'm here," Elijah said comfortingly. "Though I doubt my father'll do anything to you. He respects Danial too much."

Nice. "Why aren't you with your sister?"

Elijah rolled his eyes. "She's playing the good daughter, and spending the holiday with my father. She gets that from our mother, always wanting to please."

"That's my friend you're talking about," I growled.

"I love her, Elle. I just wish she was more independent like you."

I shrugged.

Hope bounded in, and jumped up on Elijah. He pushed her down gently, and made her sit. "What's her name?"

"Hope."

"She's cute. But she's not much of a watchdog—"

"Look, why exactly are you here, Elijah?" I interrupted. "Are you trying to be some kind of guard? Because I've got my own life, and I don't want another guard."

"Do you want a lover?" he said flatly.

I got red all the way to my ears. "What?"

"You heard me. But I'll repeat it anyway: do you want a lover like you did months ago?"

"Volunteering yourself?"

"Yes."

"You aren't cougar."

"I came prepared." He put an ocean of meaning behind his words.

I felt a rush of desire, and pushed it aside. "What do you want?"

Elijah moved faster than I could see, and then I was in his arms. I struggled, but he held me.

"I want what I've wanted since I first saw you; to be part of your life, to protect you, to make you mine." He brushed my cheek with his lips. "Do you want that?" He kissed my lips gently. "Do you want me?"

I kissed him fiercely, and then we were devouring each other's mouth. Elijah picked me up in his strong arms, and carried me into my bedroom and lay me down on the bed. Feverish with lust, I pulled off my sweater, and then my jeans. Elijah's hands were everywhere, caressing and squeezing my skin the instant I revealed it. Before long, I turned my attention to his clothes, taking off his shirt, as I kissed down his chest. He was just as muscular as he had been months ago, and the feel of all that strength beneath my fingers was such a turn-on, I began to utter soft cries of need.

When I stripped off his pants, he didn't stop me. But when I went for his underwear, he tensed up a little.

"It's okay," I said gently. "I won't hurt you."

"I've never done this," Elijah said uneasily, and swallowed. "I feel like an idiot, with you knowing more than me."

"I've never done this, either, not with another person in the flesh," I whispered, feeling only a little dishonest. "Everyone has a first time. At least ours is together."

Elijah nodded, and I eased off his underwear. The sight of his long penis engorged with blood was too much for me to withstand. A moment later, I was straddling him, moaning loudly as I eased his hard flesh into my wet and eager channel. When I began to rock on him he began to groan in pleasure, and then we were kissing, moving in tandem as fast as we could. I climaxed hard, screaming, and Elijah began moaning my name over and over as he jetted into me.

I felt him shrink, and then slip out of me. I snuggled next to him, not sure what to say. And then I swore.

"What's wrong?" Elijah said softly.

"We didn't use any protection," I grumbled.

"We don't need any," Elijah said matter-of-factly. "I'd like a child with you."

I gave him a look. "You didn't want to have sex without being Oathed before. Now you're ready to have a kid without it?"

"Give me your Oath, or I'll marry you," he said in that same calm tone. "Whichever you prefer, or both. I want to be with you, Elle."

"What if I can't have any kids?" I said in something like panic. "Female weres have a hard time conceiving. My mother did, my real mother, I mean."

Elijah rolled me to face him. "If you can't, it's okay. And you're right, I'm still uneasy about doing this, and not being tied to you officially. But I'm okay with it being on your terms, at least for now."

"What do you mean by 'for now'?"

"If you get pregnant, I'd push harder to make our relationship proper." He kissed me gently. "But I won't push, otherwise."

"Why?"

Elijah gave me an annoyed look. "Don't you want to lie here and cuddle?"

"Not until you answer me."

Elijah sat up, and ran his hand though his hair. I noticed it was longer, almost as Theo's had been, the last time I saw him. "Because I'm becoming more like a vampire," he whispered. "I can still go out in the sun and eat food. But I'm not sure how long that'll last. If I can have children at all, it'll have to be soon, before I turn completely vampire."

He looked over at me. "I don't want you to think I'm here to get a child out of you. God knows, after how my father has acted with Sarelle, I could see where you might. I'm just saying I'd like us to not do birth control. If it happens, it happens."

I considered his words. I'd never thought about having a child of my own. Did I want one? I didn't know. Would I be a good mother? *Well, I can try hard, and read up on it...*

"Do you want a child with me?" Elijah whispered. "It's okay if you don't. I will still want you the same, and for us to one day be committed to one another."

"I don't know." I sighed. "Really, I'm likely infertile, with what I know of my mom. Tawny, she tried for years with Theo and her husband. It took many years—"

"Then would you mind if we didn't use protection, for now?"

I reached down and stroked him, causing him to gasp even as he stiffened in my hand. Then I guided him into me, and we were kissing, moving frantically towards that summit until we both came together, his body so far inside mine there was not a hair's breadth between us.

"I love you," he whispered gently to me as we clutched each other, panting.

"I love you, too," I whispered back, tears in my eyes. I let out a shaky breath. "And if you want me, I'm yours."

"I do want you, Elle. And I accept your Oath." Elijah kissed me gently, and then he was rolling me over on my back, and sliding into me again with a grunt. I gave myself up completely to the feeling of rapture and ecstasy.

* * * *

The next morning, I awoke cradled in Elijah's arms. With a delicious stretch, I felt the soreness of my body and let out a little purr of contentment. That morning, for the first time, I knew a satisfaction and relaxation I'd never felt before, not since I'd become an adult. The constant tension and hunger for sex that had been such a part of me for years was suddenly missing. The relief was so good to feel that I let out another deep rumbling purr.

Elijah had indeed prepared. He'd brought a magical potion with him to change form. Just as Devlin had done in the dream, Elijah had taken every drop of my lust and need and sated it in hot flesh and slippery sweat. But the difference between my dream and this morning's reality filled my heart with joy, in that I loved Elijah, and he loved me, too. After we'd changed back to human form, Elijah had reached into his pocket, and handed me a gold choker with an eagle's head. I let him fasten it around my neck, smiling happily.

"According to were custom, we're mated now as well as Oathed," he said emotionally. "But you won't be able to take this off like your mother can take off hers, Elle."

"I had one from my Dad I used to wear for protection," I said,

87

hugging him. "It's okay. I don't want to take it off, ever."

"Today's Christmas Eve. Do you want to do anything special?"

I cringed. "I have to go and see my Dad and Mom. They're going to be at his house and my brother, too."

"Should I come?" Elijah said. "I realize I have a right to, now, but I know this is sudden. I don't want to make a scene."

"There are going to be scenes anyway," I said bitterly. I related to Elijah all of what had happened to Danial, and my mom, even some of the history I wasn't sure he knew. "They might have made up, but probably not. My dad holds a grudge really well, and my mom is the same."

"Then I'd like to come," Elijah said firmly. "I should be there for you if there's going to be fighting, even if it's just them shouting at each other."

I hugged him. "Thanks. I'd really like that."

Chapter Seven

We ended up staying in bed that morning. After letting out Hope, and feeding her, we slept away most of the day. Around five, I had some late lunch, and he had some of my soup, and a good bit of raw meat. He started to apologize, but I told him it wasn't a problem. "Raw diets are supposed to be best for weres, not a lot of processed foods. So we can eat some meat together on—" I'd been about to say "on the days you don't work." *But does he work? Has he ever?* "Are you, um, going to be home with me all the time?"

"I have a trust fund," he said. "Money isn't an issue. But I took a few classes in literature, and I'm hoping to be a playwright, if not a novelist." He made a face. "I'm told it's hard. But I want to try it." A panicked look passed over his face. "But I'll help around the house, too. I'm strong, though I admit I haven't done a lot of manual labor in my life. But you can teach me, I'm sure."

"I'll put you right to work." I kissed his cheek, and then gave his bottom a sharp pat. "But get dressed. We've got to get going."

We arrived at my Dad's house at dusk. But my father Theo opened the door instead of Danial. "Elle," he said happily. Then he noticed Elijah. "What are you doing here?"

"He's my mate," I said flatly.

My father looked like he was going to pop a gasket. "Your MATE? He's not cougar!"

"Mom's not snake, either," I announced with relish. "That doesn't seem to matter to Lash, as they are mated."

"It does matter," Theo growled. "Plus, your father-in-law hates

89

weres."

"I don't," Elijah challenged. "And what I think should matter, not my father."

Theo just looked at him, but Jenny came to the door. She looked a little tired, but she pushed my father back with enough strength that he moved a sufficient amount to let us by. "Come in," she said pleasantly. "This is a happy occasion. Welcome, Elijah."

Theo growled, but we all went into the kitchen and got some wine. After we went into the great room which I was surprised to see was missing its TV and video games.

"Danial's reclaimed the house," Theo said with a roll of his eyes. "But we can play with more people in the compound, anyway."

"Stop talking of trivialities," Jenny growled at him. "Elle, tell us of how you two met. Tell the whole story, and give us all the details!"

I told her about Elijah and his cookies, and a quick history of the pleasant moments in the past year. Though I left out Lash's saving me, and being held hostage, I could see my father suspected he'd played some pivotal part in this. But he kept quiet.

After I'd finished, Theo took Elijah for a walk to "discuss some things." And Jenny retired to her room, saying she was tired from all the decorating, and needed a nap. I nodded, thinking her lazy. As soon as she left, like magic, my mother arrived.

We baked cookies and talked a little. I wanted to bring up Elijah, but couldn't seem to find the words. Moreover, part of me wanted to tell her and Lash together when Elijah was there with me, not just her and I alone by ourselves. T and Danial arrived, in the middle of our baking.

T left for the airport after we helped him pack, and I got into a shouting match with my father, which prompted my mom to leave. When I was telling my dad where he could stick his precious business, he suddenly sniffed, and then barked out, "Who was it, Elle? Whose scent is on your skin?"

"You sound like you do with Mom," I sneered. "I don't belong to you any more than she does!"

"Answer me, Elle."

"Mine," Elijah said as he came through the doorway. "I mated her last night, and Oathed her too, Danial."

"Without my permission."

"We don't need your permission," Elijah said calmly. "I've gotten her father's permission, not that we needed that, either."

"I'm more a father to her than that cat," Danial hissed, sounding for all the world like Lash. "I'm co-Ruler with Devlin. It's custom to ask for permission if you're vampire and Oathing someone."

"Fine. May we have your permission?" Elijah said patiently. "I do respect you, Danial, and I don't want bad relations between us. But I'm also not giving up Elle."

"Why couldn't you have just fucked him?" Danial said coarsely to me. "Why did you have to mate *and* give him your Oath?"

"Because I love him."

My father's eyes bled to red. "Really? What do you know of love, either of you? You've lived a grand total of six years between you, no matter the age you look to be. Do you have any idea of the work involved in a real relationship, or how hard it is to sustain?"

"No," I said, taking Elijah's hand in mine. "We'll find out together."

"You will," he said, nodding. "I don't envy you that."

"You love Mom. Stop acting like I don't have a right to have that same kind of love for myself, Dad!"

"You have the right. What I'm against is you giving up your freedom so young to settle down without knowing anything of the world—"

"I know enough," I growled bitterly, thinking of my childhood:

guards, attacks, and my parents fighting. "And I know I want Elijah with me for the rest of my life, however long it lasts."

"As you will." Danial paused and seemed to gather himself. "Have you told your mother? I'm guessing you haven't."

"Not yet," I said. "I was waiting for…for the right moment."

"I know what you were waiting for," Danial said angrily. "To tell her and Lash together. He is not your friend, Elle."

"He saved my life," I yelled, feeling my fangs growing as I tried to keep calm. "He came to find me! He rescued me twice! You didn't!"

"So you're going to fault me for being in a coma," Danial said sarcastically.

"No, but you didn't help me when I was captured—"

"You were captured?" Elijah interjected. "When? By who?"

"When you were off nursing your wounded pride, Fool," Danial hissed at him. He turned to me, and glided over so he was right in front of me. "Who do you think let Sar know you were missing? She told Lash, and he went to look for you. But only because I noticed you weren't answering your phone, and sent Terian to look for you. When he noticed that you weren't at home, I called your mother looking for you."

Shame washed over me. "I didn't know."

"Now you do." Danial said. "Your dear Lash didn't mention me, did he?"

"He did," I said, remembering. "He said you were worried. I just didn't put the two together."

"Probably because he was trying to garner some other reward from you for saving your life and wanted full credit."

"The truth is I would've given him anything he asked for, I was so grateful," I growled. "As many times as he wanted it. But he didn't. He was a gentleman."

Elijah made a choked sound, but he didn't release my hand.

"Sickening," Danial said with distaste. "And you being cougar, too. Theo would die of shame to hear you utter those words, to know you offered yourself in such a manner. You'd think you were Sar's blood."

"I am her blood. More than I am his or yours!"

"Maybe so. Both of your mothers were sluts, and you've surpassed them."

Elijah swung at him, but Danial ducked and hit Elijah back a solid punch. Elijah fell to one knee. I helped him up, upset and angry.

"You've not fought another older vampire, have you?" Danial said maliciously to Elijah. "Practicing on weres is not good enough, Elijah. You'll have to practice harder. And I'd start soon, because I'll be calling your father tonight to tell him of your good news. I'm sure he'll want to see you shortly afterwards."

"Go ahead," Elijah said, squeezing my hand. "He's done with me and me with him."

"We'll see. And we'll see how fast the both of you survive on love when Samuel and I both cut your funding off."

I decided right then enough was enough. I walked out with Elijah, and drove us home.

Sharon was there waiting for us when we returned, Harp and Song beside her. "Is it true? Are you Oathed?"

We both said 'yes' and she gave us a hug each, telling us she was happy for us. Together, we went inside and I put on a brave face, prepared to try my best to salvage the rest of the night. But Sharon had bad news of her own to add. "Father sent me," she said hesitantly to her brother. "You are to break the Oath and return home. If you don't, Father will sever your money, and all ties."

"Tell him to go ahead," Elijah said bravely. "I'm not afraid to work for a living."

"I told him you'd say that." Sharon got up. "And he figured you would, too."

Harp grabbed hold of Elijah, and they disappeared. I let out a scream, but Sharon just faded away with Song, leaving me alone.

I tried Elijah's cell, and then Samuel's phone, but got no answer.

I sat down holding a panting, nervous Hope, and tried to think. Who could I ask for help? Danial and Theo were out; they were against the marriage, anyway. My mother could help with Lash, but was that fair to ask him for help again? And this fight wasn't against a few humans, or even a were, this was against a Ruler. What could he do, except possibly get killed. *Shit. There is only one person I can go to; I have to ask Devlin.*

Chapter Eight

I phoned Hayden that very minute, but learned Devlin and my mom and Lash were in New Orleans with Rene. I decided to just ask Lash after all, but he didn't answer his cell. So, I left messages for Devlin to call me when he got in.

He called back finally a day later. "Elle, what is it?"

"Can you come to me via demon? I need help."

"I can send Lash to you. What is it?"

"No, you."

There was silence. "Do I need to bring a chaperone?" he said finally.

"No," I answered, blushing hotly. "I need your help. I'm not going to do anything."

"You're sure? Lash let slip to me what you tried when he rescued you."

I felt white-hot anger at Lash, and growled out, "He had no right to tell you that. There's a man I love that got kidnapped. I know who has him, but I need your status to get him free."

"So Elijah came through," Devlin purred. "Good to hear. What state Ruler has him? I'll make them release him."

"His father has him."

There was a pause. "Then I can do nothing," Devlin said reluctantly. "Elijah is not one of my constituents, he's just visiting you. He never even asked me for my permission—"

I lost it. "Stop with the fucking permission!"

"Elle, I'm saying that Elijah's home is still officially Europe, and Samuel rules there, not to mention is his father. There is no law I could quote to petition for a release, especially given his biological age—"

"How about separating mates? Is there a law against that?"

Devlin paused again. "There is a law, but it's rarely enforced. Matings are easily broken. It would be better if you were Oathed—"

"We are."

"Ahh!" Devlin purred. "Then there is something I can do. Go outside and wait for me. Titus and I'll be along shortly."

"Okay." Relieved, I hung up the phone and went outside.

Five minutes later, Devlin and Titus appeared. "Take my hand."

I did, and we were instantly in Europe. We walked to the front door, a huge wooden slab easily fifteen feet high. "Why can't we go around back?" I whispered as Titus rung the bell.

"Because we are here on official business," Devlin said arrogantly. "And we are not servants."

The butler, a cowed looking man, let us in and ushered us into a sitting room. Samuel joined us a few minutes later. "Dalcon, what a surprise. What can I do for you?"

"This woman is Oathed to your son, as you no doubt know. She demands you release him, and argues that you took him here against his will."

"They are not Oathed, only mated. And my son broke that mating this morning when he bedded two young humans and one female cougar."

I felt sick, but Devlin's hand found mine, and dug his nails into my palm. I straightened with a gasp of pain.

"Be that as it may, they are Oathed," Devlin said. "And according to law, to be released from an Oath, the vampire must stand before the

96

Oathee and tell them they are free."

"That only works if the Oath is not already broken by the vampire. I think it has to be, with how my son behaved." He glanced at me. "My apologies"

"No," I said, pulling down my turtleneck to flash my choker. "I still have my choker on."

"You must be permissive, then," Samuel said in a velvety tone. "Wait here."

"Good job," Devlin whispered. "Be strong. This is going to be ugly."

Samuel returned with Elijah. But his eyes didn't look at me with love, but with scorn.

Samuel opened his mouth to speak. But before he could, Titus sprinkled something over Elijah, and Elijah went to his knees. Samuel shouted for his guards, but Titus put a barrier around us. Even as it was forming, the demons surrounding us were hammering at it, making cracks. I let out a shout, reaching for Elijah, but Titus was in the way.

"Elijah, speak the truth," Devlin said loudly. "Are you still Oathed to Elle?"

"Yes," Elijah gasped. "Yes!"

Samuel glared at Titus. "Couldn't you have left it alone?"

"You know my feelings on love spells," Titus rumbled. "Be happy you aren't feeling a spell making all your demons the object of your desire."

Samuel snarled at Titus. I helped Elijah to his feet. He leaned on me heavily for support.

"Samuel, you've tried to break up an Oathed couple," Devlin intoned. "You removed one of them to another continent and put a spell on him to hate his Oathed One. This is a serious crime, punishable—"

"Save it," Samuel interrupted angrily. "You've done worse,

Devlin."

Devlin grinned. "So I have. But I do need your word that you'll give Elijah his freedom. He is Oathed to Elle and he needs to be with her, consummating that Oath. They are one."

"Elijah is becoming vampire," Samuel said flatly. "His fertility is dwindling."

"But he is happy with her," Devlin countered. "That is what matters to him. And it should be what matters to you. Give him the freedom to choose his own fate, whatever it might be."

"Do you want children?" Samuel asked, for the first time really looking at me. "Tell the truth."

"I don't know," I said truthfully. "But we're not going to use birth control. Can that be enough?"

"Yes," Devlin finished quickly. "That can be enough for now. It is not a Ruler's place to tell his subjects they must or must not procreate."

"I agree," Samuel said grudgingly. "But I demand that Elijah and Elle spend some of their time every month with me. I have much to do, and cannot travel to see them that often."

"That is doable," Devlin said quickly, before I could answer. "Titus can teleport them."

Samuel grumbled something.

"I must get back," Devlin said firmly. "Lash is with my Oathed Ones and I'm missing the party."

I almost choked, but Samuel just nodded. "Go. We are done here."

Devlin pulled Elijah and me out the door with him and Titus teleported us to my house. Night had fallen while we'd been gone, and the fire'd gone out.

Titus helped me lay Elijah on the bed. "He'll need to sleep, but he'll be fine tomorrow." Then he disappeared.

I figured Devlin had hurried to get back to my mother and his other

Oathed One, whoever that was. Had what Seth told me in that dream about my mom been true about her? *Is she really participating in threesomes?* I pushed the thought away with revulsion, and went out, closing the door on Elijah's sleeping form.

I was surprised to see Devlin in front of the woodstove fire, fanning fresh flames. "This is a cheery home," he said as he got to his feet. "We have a woodstove now in our bedroom, did your mother tell you?"

"Don't you have to get back to Mom?" I asked, blushing.

"In due time," Devlin said, striding into my kitchen. I followed him, mystified. I saw him pour us some wine and then we sat next to the fire again. "Tell me everything."

I told him the whole story of Elijah and myself in detail, editing the sex to just that we'd had sex. Devlin listened, sipping occasionally. When I'd finished, he downed the last of his wine. "Realize that Elijah may have got one of the girls Samuel spoke of pregnant, Elle. Samuel no doubt was planning on breeding his son until that happened, so likely there's a good chance it has."

I swallowed. "I realize that."

"That child will no doubt remain with Samuel and not come to live with you. But if you aren't using any birth control, you may find yourself pregnant before long."

"My mother had a hard time conceiving."

"She was at least a decade older. But you are in your reproductive prime, Elle, as Elijah appears to be. So think heavily on what you're doing."

"I am. Danial said he wasn't going to pay any more of my bills—"

"That isn't what I'm talking about. I'm more than prepared to help out, though I'm sure Samuel will help you instead, as he seems so eager for you to get to know him now. Danial would never allow you to starve, no matter who you bedded." He paused. "Are you ready for a child? They can be time consuming, as your mother can tell you."

"I know. The truth is I'm not sure. I'm just going to take this one day at a time."

"Good. That's best." He got to his feet. "Please come and visit Sar and I in the New Year. I know you've not told Lash or her of you and Elijah, or I'd have heard of it. I'll keep it to myself until then, as will Danial."

"He's angry."

"Not at you, niece, though you're already aware of that. I'll tell him of what happened here. He's going through a lot. He'll be okay in a while."

As much as I'd hated him over the years, he'd stood up for me when it counted. So I hugged him quickly and whispered, "Thanks, Dev."

His body went rigid. I had a second to try to withdraw until he grasped me by the hair roughly and made me look at him. "What did you call me?"

"I meant Devlin—"

"Your tone was familiar."

"Dad calls you that all the time!"

"Not like that he doesn't, not with that lover's inflection—" Devlin's angry look melted to utter horror and then he went to his knees, bringing me along with him.

"You were there, weren't you?" he said in a cracked voice. "In that dream, that night. Tell me if you were."

"I don't know what you're talking about!" I said desperately.

"SAY IT!" he shouted, his eyes pits of volcanic fire, melting gold and flame.

"I was," I whispered.

Devlin drew a ragged breath. "For how much…of the dream?"

"For all of it. Since the beginning when you were mortal…to when you killed me."

His arms tightened so much I spasmed in his grip, feeling my ribs cracking. And then he eased up and I drew a long, gasping breath. "Are you going to kill me now?" I whispered. "Because I remember it?"

Devlin shuddered, and I struggled to escape him, sure he meant to hurt me. Then I noticed he was sobbing. "No. I'm sorry," he said brokenly. "I'm so sorry."

I held still in his arms as he sobbed. Finally, he got control of himself, though he didn't let me go. "Please forgive me. I never wanted anything to happen between us to scare you. That's another reason I refused you. And I'll be punishing Leri, as it must be she who allowed this—"

"I asked for it," I whispered. "There's no point punishing her."

"I'm at a loss for words," Devlin whispered. "I haven't been in many years. But what can I possibly say to make things okay between us?" He drew back and looked at me critically. "Do you want a forgetting spell?"

"Are you going to take one? Because I always remembered all of it, and just dealt with it, this past year."

"No." He let out a breath. "I enjoyed what we did. But I'd appreciate you not telling your mother or Lash. I've no wish to get cut off or cut up." He bit his lip with one fang. "And know I meant what I said about real life and dreams. I'd never have done what I did to you if I'd known you were there with me."

"More's the pity," I said, trying to both be adult and make light of the horror of the dream. "Parts of the dream were good."

"Yes, they were," Devlin purred, his lips curving in a smile. "Your young man will be enthused that you are so open-minded. Tell him I'm willing to teach him some tricks, if he's open to learning."

Not going to happen. "Thanks," I said awkwardly. "I appreciate you helping me."

"That's what uncles are for," he said pointedly. "Lock your door."

He walked out, and a moment later Titus appeared, and teleported him.

I went back to my sleeping Elijah, and cuddled up beside him. *I'm in love, we're going to have a family, and we're going to be together. I'm finally free of everything—loneliness, fear, shyness, rage, and lust—that my whole life I've felt trapped by. The truth is those feelings never had any hold over me, none of them. I just needed to be myself, and believe that that was enough of a reason to be loved.*

I closed my eyes, thinking about the good days to come. In a few moments, I fell asleep.

The End

About the author

Tara Fox Hall's writing credits include nonfiction, horror, suspense, action-adventure, erotica, and contemporary and historical paranormal romance. She is the author of the paranormal action-adventure *Lash* series and the vampire romantic suspense *Promise Me* series. Tara divides her free time unequally between writing novels and short stories, chainsawing firewood, caring for stray animals, sewing cat and dog beds for donation to animal shelters, and target practice.

www.tarafoxhall.com

Other works by the author with Melange Books, LLC

Return To Me
Surrender to Me
The Origin of Fear in Spellbound 2011 Anthology
Night Music in Midnight Thirsts II Anthology
Partners in Midnight Thirsts II Anthology
Kink in Wicked Christmas Wishes Anthology
The Oath in Wicked Christmas Wishes Anthology
Bedtime Shadows Anthology
Make Me Behave Anthology
Latham's Landing, An Anthology
The Oath
Her Frozen Heart, in Frozen Anthology
Night Music, a Novella

The Promise Me Series
Promise Me, Book 1
Broken Promise, Book 2
Taken in the Night, Book 3
Taken for his Own, Book 4
Promise Me Anthology, Book 4.5
Immortal Confessions, Book 5
Her Secret, Book 6
Point of No Return, Book 7
Lost Paradise, Book 8
Dark Solace, Book 9
Eye of the Storm, Book 10
Tempest of Vengeance, Book 11

www.ingramcontent.com/pod-product-compliance
Lightning Source LLC
Chambersburg PA
CBHW020412150626
46554CB00013B/830